031457

TAYLOR, A.

Double exposure

DOUBLE EXPOSURE

Andrew Taylor

Lions
An Imprint of HarperCollins*Publishers*

First published in the U.K. in 1990 in Armada
This Lions edition first published in 1992

Lions is an imprint of
HarperCollins Children's Books, a division of
HarperCollins Publishers Ltd,
77–85 Fulham Palace Road,
Hammersmith, London W6 8JB

Printed and bound in Great Britain by
HarperCollins Manufacturing, Glasgow

exposure *n.* **1.** the act of exposing or the condition of being exposed . . .

double exposure *n.* **1.** the act or process of recording two superimposed images on a photographic medium, usually done intentionally to produce a special effect. **2.** The photograph resulting from such an act.

Collins Dictionary of the English Language, 1979.

CHAPTER ONE

I fell out of the train and into a nightmare.

Nothing fancy. Not even frightening – just embarrassing. Totally, paralysingly, cringingly embarrassing. The sort of embarrassment that makes a bit of straightforward terror seem quite attractive.

I'd done the final leg of the journey on one of those little local trains that look like a cross between an overgrown bus and a mobile dustbin. The train was running late and I kept glancing at my watch. Maybe Smith had already given up in disgust. Maybe she'd had an accident on the way to the station. Maybe she was having second thoughts about inviting me down. I had a new haircut, new clothes and all the old worries. I admit it: where Smith is concerned I'm not entirely rational.

The train slid along the platform and stopped. I tried to pull back the catch on the door. It wouldn't budge. I swore. No one else was getting off. No one was getting on. No sign of Smith. I pulled down the window and, leaning against the door, groped for the outside handle. The strap of the camera round my neck was doing its best to strangle me. I twisted the handle and that wouldn't move either. My armpits were getting clammy.

Suddenly the handle gave way. The door opened. It had most of my weight behind it so I went with it. The bag over my shoulder swung me further off balance. I fell out of the train and on to the platform, rolling in a desperate attempt to protect the camera.

I collided with a pair of legs, which were slightly softer than the surface of the platform. They were a woman's legs, I noticed. She keeled over and joined me on the ground. I heard laughter from the train and running feet along the platform. I looked up and there was Smith sprinting towards me.

"Sorry," I said to the woman.

"I should think so too," she snapped. She was about 35, a blonde with a carrying voice.

Smith stopped a couple of yards away. "Hi," she said.

The woman stood up and dusted herself down. "Is this – ?"

"This is Chris Dalham," Smith said. "And Chris, this is Frances Byram."

"Ah," I said. "Hi."

I wished I could get back into the train and shut the door and play the whole scene again. Instead I sat up, cradling the camera. A tall man loped along the platform towards us. He had brown, crinkly hair and a wrinkled face like a sad monkey's.

"This is Chris," Smith said to him.

He stuck out his hand in my direction. I thought he meant me to shake it. He hauled me to my feet so vigorously that the bag flew off my shoulder. Smith picked it up and handed it to me.

"I'm Drew," he said. "You've met Frances already, I guess."

He had a nice smile and bloodshot eyes that had once been like his daughter's. His accent was more obviously American than hers.

"In a manner of speaking." Frances glanced at him, ignoring me completely. "Did you get the Perrier?"

He nodded. "There's a deli behind the church. It's got some amazing cheeses."

"Good," Frances said. "Then we might as well be off."

She marched down the platform with Drew beside her. If she'd been a kettle she'd have boiled herself dry by now. Smith and I followed. She didn't look at me and I didn't look at her.

It was weird. I'd been thinking and dreaming of this meeting for nearly two months. I'd rehearsed all these conversations in my head. I'd worked out a dozen opening gambits, a dozen replies. All of them witty as hell, all of them meaning more than they said. I thought I'd covered all the possible situations.

But I hadn't. I'd forgotten Smith's father and his current girlfriend. Not exactly forgotten them: I knew they'd be there, of course; but I kind of assumed they'd be in the background. Shadowy figures that wouldn't have much to do with me and Smith.

As I said, it was a stupid little nightmare. The only thing that made it hard to handle was the fact that it was real.

Frances unlocked the driver's door of a black Peugeot 205, the model with the 1.9-litre engine. Drew put my bag and his shopping in the boot. Smith and I scrambled into the back. Our elbows touched.

She moved half an inch away from me. "Have you had lunch?" she said.

"I had a couple of sandwiches in the buffet."

"I'll fix you something at the cottage if you want."

"That's okay."

"Dinner won't be till around eight."

Quite a conversation. Sparkling. Crammed with emotional undercurrents. We stared glumly out of opposite windows as Frances drove out of the station car park.

Drew turned round and said to me: "It's about five miles to the cottage. Has Smith told you about it?"

So even her father called her that. Smith has this thing about her first name. She doesn't want anyone to know what it is.

"We only got there on Saturday," Smith said. Today was Monday.

"Yeah. Well, it's in the middle of nowhere. It's a converted water mill – old as the hills. The only other building in sight is a farmhouse, and that's derelict."

"Youlgreave Barton," Frances said to no one particular. "Essentially it's the cross-wing of a medieval manor house, with later additions. The mill is roughly contemporary, perhaps a little later."

Smith glanced upwards. I knew as clearly as if she'd said it that what she was thinking was *Here we go again*.

"The nearest village is on the other side of the hill," Drew went on. "Quanton St John. Picture postcard stuff. You'll see it in a moment. Just a pub and a church and a few cottages."

"And that wretched housing estate," Frances said. "The planning committee that passed that scheme should be hunted down and shot."

"People have got to live somewhere," Smith said.

By now we were out of the town. There wasn't much to see – green fields, a few trees and stone walls, the odd cow and an awful lot of sky.

"Up there," Drew said, pointing at the window beside me, "that's Oscar's Castle."

I looked, expecting to see a ruined tower or something. A track led off the road and up the side of the hill. Near the skyline was a huddle of huts and a few tents. There were washing lines and a couple of rusting cars. People were moving around in the field below. No doubt they were sowing or reaping or ploughing or whatever.

"Gypsies?" I said.

"It's a sort of commune," Drew said. "Alternative lifestyles and organic farming."

"Elderly hippies," Frances said. "The great unwashed. Parasites. They're pretending to opt out of society."

"Not parasites," Smith said. "A guy I talked to said they bought the land."

"I imagine most of them are drawing social security."

"Why's it called a castle?" I said, not because I wanted to know but because I sensed that Frances and Smith were on a collision course and thought someone should try to divert them.

10

"According to local legend it's the site of a prehistoric encampment," Frances said. "But there's no archaeological confirmation of that."

She changed down to overtake a tractor on the outskirts of the picture-postcard village. On the other side of the village we turned off the B road and on to a lane that snaked round the bottom of the hill called Oscar's Castle. It was single-track and a ribbon of rough grass had pushed itself up through the tarmac in the middle.

"You don't get many cars here," Frances said with obvious satisfaction as we bumped along. "Just the occasional tractor."

"And hordes of cattle," Smith said.

I'd already guessed that from the surface of the road.

We stopped at a five-bar gate. Drew got out and opened it. Frances drove into a cobbled yard beyond. A cottage built of pink and grey stones straggled round two sides of it. There was a stream on the third side and a low hedge, broken by the gate, on the fourth.

Frances got out of the car, looked around and inhaled deeply.

Smith whispered in my ear: "She's *breathing* it. It's called the perfume of antiquity."

Drew unlocked the front door and elbowed it open. We walked straight into a long living room. The furniture was old and looked as if it had come down in the world. There was a faded rug on the floor. No TV, but a portable stereo tape recorder was on a table near the door. At the far end was a fireplace so big you could have roasted an elephant in it.

It was a warm day but the house felt freezing. I mean, let's face it, stone-flagged floors, two-feet thick walls and tiny windows may have seemed the height of luxury in the Middle Ages, but things have changed a bit since then.

"Why don't you show your friend round?" Frances said to Smith.

There wasn't much to see. In the other part of the

11

ground floor there was a loo and a kitchen, plus a dank, walk-in larder like an economy-class medieval prison cell. Drew lugged the shopping into the kitchen and filled the kettle.

"That's where the mill used to be," Frances called after us.

The stairs were stone and built into the thickness of the wall. On the first floor were three bedrooms – a double and two singles – and a bathroom. There was also an outside staircase of stone that went from the yard to the double bedroom, which had once been a hayloft.

"Don't forget to show him the exposed timbers in our room," Frances shouted. "The truss probably came from Youlgreave Barton. I think it's older than the house itself."

I thought a truss was something you wore when you had a hernia. Smith, her face blank, opened the door of the double bedroom and silently jerked her thumb at the ceiling. There were some wormy old beams up there.

"Great," I said politely. "Which is the truss?"

"God knows," Smith said, and shut the door.

Our rooms were much smaller. Each had just a single bed, a chest of drawers and hard chair. I dumped my bag on the chair and the camera on the chest of drawers.

"You still take a lot of photos?" Smith said.

I nodded.

"Tea's ready," Frances shouted.

Smith muttered something under her breath and led the way downstairs. In the kitchen Frances was setting out cups and saucers of delicate-looking green and white china on the table. Then she poured the tea and passed me a cup.

To my horror it was black. Huge tea leaves floated on the surface. They were like waterlogged flies.

"There's lemon if you want it," Frances said. "Personally I find it ruins the flavour."

"Could I have some sugar?" I said faintly.

"Sugar?"

Honest, you'd have thought I'd asked for arsenic. Frances made a great fuss out of looking for it. Smith found a packet at the back of one of the cupboards. I put in three spoonfuls. Even so, the tea tasted foul.

"Come on," Smith said, "we'll have ours outside."

We went out into the yard and sat on a low wall by the stream. Smith put her cup down on the wall. I looked at mine and winced.

For the first time she smiled at me. "Frances is educating our palates," she said. "This is Lapsang Souchong. All the way from China. Wow."

"Can they see us from the house?" I said.

She shook her head. We lifted our cups and flicked the contents into the stream.

"We've got three or four hours till dinner," she said. "What do you want to do?"

I looked at her. "What *is* there to do around here?"

"Good question. We eat and drink, and that takes up a lot of time with Frances around. She's a cordon bleu cook, you know? Naturally. Aside from that, if it's raining, we sit inside and read a book. If it's not, we go for a walk."

"Great," I said. "So we go for a walk."

"Great," she said with a similar lack of enthusiasm.

I fetched my camera automatically. I feel undressed without it.

"You're going for a walk?" Frances said.

"How did you guess?" Smith said. "Where's my father?"

"Upstairs. Working."

"What a surprise."

Smith and I wandered down the lane, picking our way in single file through the cow pats. It was a golden summer evening and the sun's warmth made everything smell like a farmyard. There were a lot of flies and midges too.

High, unkempt hedges on either side of the lane cut off most of the view.

At first we didn't talk. I had all these things I'd planned to say to Smith but she'd put up a barrier round herself and I couldn't get through. I guessed she was miserable, and I wasn't exactly happy myself.

After a couple of hundred yards she stopped beside an iron gate that was propped across a gap in the hedge. A hand-painted notice was tied on to the bars. TRESPASS-ERS WILL BE PROSECUTED.

"That's Youlgreave Barton," she said.

We leant on the gate and stared across a wilderness of nettles and brambles at the house. It was T-shaped and built of crumbling stone. All the windows were different sizes and on different levels; and the lower ones had been boarded up. The house looked as though no one had planned it – as though it had just grown and lived like a person. And now it was dying.

Smith shivered. "This place gives me the creeps. I bet it's haunted."

"Rubbish," I said. "Ghosts are all in the mind."

I opened the camera case and took out the camera and the light meter.

"You figure that's worth a picture?"

"I've got one shot left," I said. "I'm doing a double-exposed film. It's a sort of experiment."

"Double-exposed? What does that mean?"

"Two photographs on one negative – one on top of the other." I had the camera open now and was sizing up the picture. I was too far away: I wanted to frame the big window at the end of the house, the one that was covered with corrugated iron with the crooked line of smaller windows above. "I'm going in. No one's going to mind, are they?"

"Why should they?"

Something in Smith's voice told me that she minded. She really did think the place was spooky.

"Let's go somewhere else," I said. "I can take another photo."

"Come on." She was already climbing the gate.

I followed her over. There was a path of sorts leading up to the house – so overgrown we could have done with a machete or two, or maybe a bulldozer. The air was very still and hot: the hedges and the house itself acted as wind-breaks. The heat and the silence pressed down on us.

Smith said, "It's like no one's ever been here before," and I knew what she meant.

I found the spot I wanted about thirty feet away from the big window. The sun slanted through the branches of a dead tree on to the side of the house, making broad bars of shadow like a gigantic spider's web. I like taking pictures in the early evening: you get these incredible contrasts. Smith leant against a chunk of stone while I fiddled with the light meter and set the aperture and the shutter speed.

"This was a garden once," she said. "That was a lawn, and they had roses over there. This thing I'm leaning on used to be a sundial." Her voice sharpened. "What's that?"

"What's what?"

"I thought I heard something moving."

I shrugged, concentrating on the camera. "Maybe it was a rabbit."

I pressed the shutter. Smith watched me putting away the camera in its case.

"You take it really seriously, don't you?" she said. "Photography, I mean."

"Well," I said awkwardly. "If you're going to do it at all, you – "

Something snarled behind us. No words – just this roar of rage. Smith grabbed my hand, or maybe I grabbed hers.

The snarl translated itself into words.

"And what the hell do you think you're doing?"

Smith gave a gasp. The sort of noise you make when someone punches you in the stomach.

We swung round. A man was standing five yards behind us. He'd just come round the corner of the house and he was waving a stick in our direction. Smith sighed – with relief, I think. Whoever he was, he wasn't a ghost.

"I presume," he said, "you can read?"

He was an old bloke in a baggy, off-white suit. On his head was a Panama hat with a broken brim. His face was flushed with the heat and maybe with anger. A wispy moustache perched on his upper lip, giving him a vaguely military air. But round his neck was a clergyman's dog-collar.

"Or perhaps you can't read?" he went on. "It wouldn't surprise me, given the deficiencies of modern education."

He wasn't snarling any more. His voice was clipped – and so controlled that you got the impression that only sheer willpower stopped him from biting our ankles.

Smith and I spoke at the same time.

"If you mean that notice – " she began.

"Look, we weren't doing any harm – "

"This is private property. If I catch you here again, you'll regret it."

"Okay . . . sorry." I tried to pull Smith down the path towards the gate. "We were just going, honest."

He slashed the stick like a sabre. "I could sue you for trespass."

Smith's chin went up. "You'd have to prove criminal damage. Aren't you overreacting a bit?"

The clergyman turned a darker shade of red and made an explosive noise that sounded like *Gorwhumphah*. I

16

pulled Smith halfway down the path. He advanced after us. It looked as if we were about to face a one-man Charge of the Light Brigade.

"Don't you play the barrack-room lawyer with *me*, young lady," he said. "Or – *Gorwhumphah*."

"Come *on*," I said to Smith.

She pulled her hand away from mine, gave the clergy-man one of those put-down stares I remembered so well, and strolled down the path to the gate. The old man stood watching us while we climbed over. As we walked on down the lane, out of his field of vision, I heard one last *Gorwhumphah* behind us. I grinned and looked at Smith. To my surprise she was trembling.

"Hey," I said. "It's okay. You were great."

"That guy makes me so angry," she muttered fiercely. "Who does he think he is? It's so unnecessary."

"That's his problem," I said, "not ours. So much for brotherly love and the peace that passes all understanding."

"He's a hypocrite. *And* sarcastic. Sarcasm is the lowest form of wit."

"And I expect he drinks on the quiet too. Keeps a crate of whisky under the pulpit."

It wasn't very funny but she giggled. We walked on for another hundred yards.

"Where do we go now?" I said.

"If we continue along here, we get to Quanton St John. But it's at least a mile away. Or we can go across the fields and loop back to the Mill."

She stopped by another gate and pointed. There was a field on the other side and it was full of cows. One of them was only a few yards away. It raised its head and looked at me. Maybe it was a young bull. Who cared? The point was, it had a vicious looking pair of horns and it was huge.

"See that ridge beyond the field?" Smith said. "Oscar's Castle's on the other side."

"Why don't we walk back up the lane?" I said, sort of casually. "It'll be quicker. I'm thirsty."

Smith looked at me and I had an uncomfortable feeling that I hadn't spoken quite casually enough.

"Okay," she said. "More Lapsang?"

"Water will do." At least Frances couldn't muck that up.

So we turned round. The Rabid Reverend seemed to have vanished. For a while we walked in a silence I didn't know how to break.

At last I said: "What do you think of Paul Anders, then?" I'd sent her tapes of the first and third albums at the end of last month.

"He's good," she said. "Kind of grows on you, doesn't he? You have to work on it."

"Right. I've got some more tapes in my bag. The second and fourth albums."

"Great," she said. "We can play them to Frances."

"She likes Paul Anders? Come off it."

"It'll do her good," Smith said. "Education's a two-way process."

"You know Paul Anders is on tour at present?"

A shake of her head.

"They say he's really good, live. He's got a new lead guitarist in the backing band." I paused and swallowed. Why the hell was she making me so nervous? "I'm trying to get two tickets for Saturday night. Would you come?"

She slowed down, then stopped. Her eyes slid up and met mine. Blue eyes with sort of greeny flecks in them. "In London?"

I nodded. "He's doing four gigs at the Palace in Willesden. But I don't know if we can get tickets. It's booked solid. Clive's handling it for me."

"Your sister's boyfriend, right? The one your parents don't like."

The fact that Smith had bothered to remember gave me a little rush of pleasure. "Judith doesn't like him either,

18

just now," I said. "She thinks he ought to settle down and get a proper job. And he said he hadn't got the time. So she said he could have the ring back. And now Clive's trying to make it up to her by getting Paul Anders tickets for me."

"I guess Clive isn't much of a psychologist," Smith said. "Saturday, you say?"

I nodded. "We could go up on the train together." I was due to go home on Saturday. The rest of them were staying until the following week.

"It would mean a night in London," she said.

"Yeah. We could stay at Clive's. He's got lots of room." Honesty made me add: "It'd probably mean sleeping bags on the floor."

"Uh huh."

"Or maybe your dad would let you use your flat. Or even let *us*."

"Getting away from Frances," Smith said slowly, "would be heaven."

"It's that bad?"

"Worse. Dad's had some pretty weird girlfriends before but Frances . . ."

Her voice tailed off and she stared at the ground. We were standing in the middle of the lane among the cow pats.

"Would he let you go?" I said.

"I'm not sure." She shrugged and started walking again. "I'll think about it."

Where does that leave me, I wondered? Maybe she thought I was pushing her too far, too quickly. Maybe her dad wouldn't let her come. Hell, maybe Clive wouldn't get the tickets. Clive's a nice guy but his worst enemy wouldn't call him reliable.

Smith looked over her shoulder. "But thanks. It's a great idea. I'd really like to see Paul Anders."

* * *

19

"You're back early," Frances said.

She was in the kitchen, making a gigantic salad in a wooden bowl. Salad bores me rigid. Rabbit food.

"Chris wants some water," Smith said.

Frances raised her eyebrows as though I'd demanded a large gin and tonic.

"I'll get it," I said quickly. "Where do you keep the glasses?"

I was too late. Frances put down the knife with a clatter, got a glass from the cupboard and the Perrier water from the fridge. I'd been wrong. Given half a chance, Frances could muck up even the water. I tried to look grateful. Carbonated mineral water gives me hiccups. Besides, I can't see the point in paying for something you can get for free out of the tap; and tap water's much nicer too.

"Where did you go?" Frances asked.

"Down to Youlgreave Barton," Smith said.

"You didn't go in the garden, did you? It's private."

I hiccupped.

"Not for long," Smith said. "We met this bizarre clergyman who seemed to think we were housebreakers."

Frances turned away to wash a carrot under the tap. "Elderly, was he? That's Mr Gisburn, the Rector. I hope you didn't upset him."

"It was like more the other way round. That guy's mentally unbalanced."

"He's the local representative for the Keystone Trust," Frances went on as if she hadn't heard. "I think he's on the national committee too. They own Youlgreave Barton as well as the Mill. They haven't been able to renovate it yet but they have to be very careful about whom they allow there."

"We weren't planning on vandalizing it," Smith said.

"That's not the point. The building's in a dangerous state, and of course there's always the risk of accidental damage."

20

"What's the Keystone Trust?" I said, just before Smith exploded.

"It's a charity that rescues buildings – historic buildings that would otherwise decay or be demolished." She was cutting the carrot very quickly into very small pieces. "And they rent them to people like us, people who appreciate them, to raise income for their work."

People like us? That was a laugh.

"I see," said Smith. "And what about people who aren't like us? They wave a stick at them and prosecute them for trespass, huh?"

"Don't be silly, dear. Now, perhaps you and Chris would like to help? The table needs laying, for example, and one of you could peel the potatoes."

Smith's face was white, and her eyes looked vast. I'd seen her angry before, but never quite like this.

"But don't make too much noise, will you?" Frances went on, unaware of the effect she was having. "Your father's working."

Smith whirled round and left the kitchen.

It turned into one of those evenings you prefer to forget as quickly as possible.

During dinner Frances talked improvingly – about art and music and architecture and literature; it was like being back at school. Her voice went on and on. She was as impossible to ignore as a dripping tap.

Drew, who came out of their bedroom just before the meal, wasn't any use as a diversion: his head was still full of the report he was writing, and he didn't say much.

I had my own problems. The food was unlike anything I'd ever eaten before. Each time I put something in my mouth I had no idea what my tastebuds were going to do with it. Then there was the cutlery. I mean, when you're given three knives and two forks, which pair are you supposed to use? I also ran into difficulties with something called a globe artichoke, but I won't go into that.

After the pudding there was a lull in the lecture. Frances glanced out of the window, which overlooked Oscar's Castle.

"It reminds me of Africa," she said – quietly for her; she was looking at Drew.

"What does?" he said gently.

She shrugged. "I don't know. The quality of the evening light, I think."

"Which part of Africa would that be?" Smith said. "It's a big place."

"Rhodesia. I – I was born there."

Frances was still looking out of the window but I don't think she was seeing Oscar's Castle or an English evening.

"I thought they called it Zimbabwe now."

It wasn't what Smith said, it was the way she said it. She put on this exaggerated British accent, especially on the "a" of "Zimbabwe".

"Have some cheese, Chris," Drew said to me in a grim voice that meant he wanted to change the subject and wasn't going to take no for an answer.

I couldn't figure out what was happening, besides the obvious fact that Smith was trying to needle Frances. There were six sorts of cheese and they all looked disgusting.

"Try the Double Border Cheddar," Frances said mechanically; she still sounded as though she were several thousand miles away from us. "It's quite marvellous."

"No thanks, I'm full," I said, which was a lie.

"Yuk," Smith said, looking at the cheeseboard. "Are all Double Border Cheddars matured for six hundred years?"

Drew looked at her: he'd caught the sneer in her voice. Just as he was about to say something, the miracle happened.

Frances pushed back her chair. "Do you mind if I leave you with the washing up? I've got a splitting headache. I think I'll go to bed."

She fended off Drew's attempts to force-feed her with painkillers, Lapsang and Drinking Chocolate.

"It's just the sunshine," she said. "Sleep's the only cure, darling. I'll be fine in the morning."

I'd expected the atmosphere would lighten once she'd gone upstairs. I hoped that maybe Smith would mention the Paul Anders concert to Drew. Ah well. In the event we washed up in almost complete silence. I was in the middle of a wordless family quarrel. It didn't take much intelligence to work out that Frances was the cause.

Over coffee Smith read a magazine while I looked at the Keystone Trust's folder of information about the Mill and the surrounding area.

"I guess I'll do some more work," Drew said.

Smith didn't look up. "Uh huh."

"Down here. I don't want to disturb Frances. Maybe you guys would like to go to bed. It's been a long day."

"Okay," Smith said, still not looking at him. "If that's what you want."

Wow, I thought, these Keystone Trusties really know how to enjoy themselves.

Drew settled himself on the sofa with a small mountain of files beside him. He's a big wheel in the R & D department of an American-based electronics company. He's been loaned to the British subsidiary, which is why he and Smith are living in the UK.

We washed up the coffee things and trailed upstairs. Smith muttered good night and disappeared into the bathroom. I went into my bedroom, which felt like a prison cell. It was 10.30. I wanted to put a new film in the camera but I found I couldn't do that because I'd left all my new films at home. Typical. A great omen for my future career as a world-class photographer.

I turned out the light but I couldn't sleep. The darkness and the silence were like a pair of blankets over my face. After a while I sat on the end of the bed and looked out of the open window. It wasn't really dark – more a sort of grey; it was the absence of artificial lights that was unsettling. My window overlooked the yard, part of the lane and the field on the other side. Gradually I realized that it wasn't really quiet either. Things were rustling out there. All the invisible inhabitants of the countryside.

I don't mind admitting I was feeling low. I'd been looking forward to today for so long. The higher your hopes, the further they can fall. It wasn't just Frances and Drew. It was Smith herself. Before now, we'd spent less than two days together. We'd been by ourselves and we'd got to know each other fast because we'd had no choice. Drew had been wrongfully arrested, someone had got killed, and Smith and I had been on the run. We'd had everyone against us. We couldn't have been more alone if we'd been marooned on a desert island.

Now we were back in the real world and everything was different. In the real world Smith was a person with a family and background. An American girl who went to an English boarding school; a person whose father didn't have to worry about money; who knew which knife to use and how to eat an artichoke.

I didn't fit. I was beginning to think she didn't really want me here at all. I was just an embarrassment. In her world I stuck out like a black face under a copper's helmet. As far as I could see, I had only one thing going in my favour: I was someone she could moan to about Frances.

I don't know how long I stayed by the window. My skin grew cold. Once I heard something snuffling, like something trying to conceal the fact that they were crying. Probably it was the mating call of the weasel or a cow's digestive system in overdrive. But it sounded like crying.

Then there was a different sound: footsteps coming softly up the lane.

A passing yokel, I thought. Or the Rabid Rector on Night Patrol. But the footsteps stopped at the gate to the yard.

Someone was standing there. He was a darker grey against the grey of the lane behind. A few seconds later, he climbed over the gate. He moved very slowly and carefully.

For an instant my mind was a blank. Then the thoughts crowded in. The gate wasn't locked. You'd only climb over it if you didn't want to make a noise, if you didn't want the latch to click and hinges to squeak. It had to be a burglar or maybe a car thief. But surely Drew was still downstairs?

I slithered off the bed. I needed to tell someone – Drew or Smith? The intruder was cutting across the yard towards the flight of steps that led up to the double bedroom.

At that moment Smith went into the bathroom and closed the door. A wedge of yellow light spilled through the frosted glass and across the cobbles. The shadow broke into a run. Too late. I'd seen who it was.

So why was Frances behaving like a criminal?

CHAPTER THREE

"I think," Frances said, "we might get more from *Don Giovanni*. Mozart can really be most amusing, you know."

Smith wasn't giving up that easily. "But how do you know Paul Anders isn't 'most amusing' too?"

"Well, it's pop music, isn't it? Very limited, almost by definition."

"I don't know if it's pop music exactly," I said, seething quietly. "Paul Anders has never had a chart hit."

"You'll grow out of it, Chris. Sacharine tunes. The three-chord trick. Adolescent lyrics. Mindless rhythms."

She half turned as she said that, and gave me a toothy smile. I squirmed in the back seat of the Peugeot. Smith was beside Frances in the front. It was Tuesday morning and no way was Paul Anders going to be part of the in-car entertainment. I guess Smith only suggested it to stir things up.

Unruffled, Frances fed a cassette into the tape deck. The music at least had the advantage of killing the conversation. Frances liked her Mozart as loud as possible. Fortunately it was only a short journey. Drew needed to work; and Frances had decided we'd go into the town, do some shopping and take in a few of the architectural glories on offer. It sounded quite a programme. I had my own plans.

We passed the station on our way into the centre, and I looked almost longingly at it. That way was London and sanity. The simple life. Ordinary, dirty streets, lots of people and a total absence of cows.

But no Smith. I stared at the back of her neck and thought I'd never known before how you could be close to someone and so far away at the same time. She'd had her dark hair cut short since I last saw her. It suited her.

Frances parked in the main street. "Now – do you want to come with me? I'm going to look round the Abbey."

"I figured on doing some shopping," Smith said. "Maybe I'll give the Abbey a miss."

"Me too," I said quickly, wondering if Smith was expecting me to go round the church with Frances.

Frances sighed to show how disappointed she was with us and arranged to meet us at the car in an hour and a half.

Smith stared after her as she strode along the pavement.

"What does she do for a living?" I said.

"Eh? Oh, she's a lawyer. Tell me something, do *you* find her attractive?"

I blinked. It was the last thing I'd expected Smith to say. But there's a lot to be said for American directness. It saves time.

"Yeah, well – I suppose if you like older women . . . I mean there's nothing wrong with her physically, is there? The problems start when she opens her mouth."

I knew I was flushing. I thought I'd really blown it with Smith, now and for ever. But she wanted an answer and I wasn't going to start telling her lies.

"No sense of humour," she said. "Have you noticed?"

I nodded.

"The sensitivity of a cockroach. Snobbish, too – you remember yesterday? *People like us* . . . Made me want to throw up. I shouldn't have asked you to visit, not while she's around. I'm sorry."

"Hey – it's okay. I'd have come anyway."

She nearly smiled. Then: "I don't know what my father sees in her."

"That's his business, isn't it?" Which was true but not what she wanted to hear. So I hurried on: "Did you know she went out last night, after she'd gone up to bed?"

Smith was interested all right, but she wasn't impressed when she heard what I'd seen.

"So? She had a headache, remember. Maybe she just went out to clear her head. Didn't want to disturb Dad.'

"Maybe. But she seemed so furtive about it."

"You're crazy," Smith said. "What do you think she was doing? Meeting a boyfriend or something?"

Put like that, it sounded stupid. I let it ride and said I wanted to buy some films and maybe get one developed.

"Your double exposures? What's the point of two pictures on one negative?"

I explained that it was meant to be artistic. I was trying to make a dream sequence by putting the same black-and-white film twice through the camera. The first time round I'd taken shots of clouds, ripples on water, the branches of trees: I wanted those for background. The second time I concentrated on strong images, like the windows and the shadows on the wall at Youlgreave Barton.

"Sounds a bit arty-farty if you ask me," Smith said.

I shrugged. "I just wanted to see what would happen."

We ambled up the street, looking for a photographer's. If you can, it's always worth buying and developing films through a professional: it costs a bit more than using mail order or going to a chainstore, but the results are usually better and you've got more comeback if they aren't.

On our way we passed the Abbey and the row of old houses that faced it across a green.

"Step on it," Smith said suddenly. "There's Frances."

I glanced across the grass. Frances was only thirty yards away, beside an ornate gatehouse in the middle of the row of houses. She was facing away from us and talking to someone I couldn't see, because he was standing in the shadow under the archway.

We accelerated past the church and took the next left. As we rounded the corner, I looked back. The man had come out of the shadow and for a second I saw him quite well. He was wearing a torn yellow tee-shirt and jeans.

28

His hair was long and red; it dangled in a pony tail down his back. He and Frances were shaking hands.

"Hey, wait," I said to Smith. "She's saying how-do-you-do to a hippie."

Smith stopped. "Are you sure?" She peered round the corner. "No, she's not. She's not even there any more."

"Well, she was." I stared across the green. "They must have gone through the gateway together."

"She's not the type to go slumming."

I nodded. "Probably just buying cocaine."

Smith smiled absent-mindedly and walked on down the side street. She was looking past me, across the street. "Is that the sort of place you want?"

It was a double-fronted shop with the paint peeling off its door and a sign above the windows saying RONALD RAYNE PHOTOGRAPHER. We crossed the road. In one window there were two shelves of secondhand cameras gathering dust. In the other was a selection of photographs. There were bouncing brides, sweating bridegrooms and bulging babies: the professional's bread and butter. All of the photographs were slightly bleached by the sun and surrounded by dead flies in various stages of decomposition.

"It'll do," I said.

I pushed open the door. A bell clanked above my head: a weary, almost apologetic sound that somehow went with the dead flies and faded photographs.

An elderly man with wide shoulders was stooping behind the glass-topped counter. He looked up, frowning. It might have been at my new haircut or maybe the shirt I was wearing; people his age usually find something to frown at when I walk in. His eyes were watery, and he wriggled his shoulders as though he were flexing a pair of wings.

"Yes," he said in a voice that wasn't exactly designed to win friends and influence people, let alone attract potential customers.

"Do you stock one-twenty film?' I asked.

He nodded. His eyes strayed down to the leather case that hung from my shoulder and I thought there might have been a gleam of interest in them.

"Colour or black and white?" he said.

"Two of each, please. What speeds have you got?"

A tear ran down Mr Rayne's cheek. He brushed it away. We had a little technical discussion about film speeds, during which he became almost matey. Smith wandered round the shop, examining more examples of Mr Rayne's work. At last he allowed his curiosity to triumph.

"One-twenty? That's quite unusual these days. I always say medium format sorts the men from the boys, hah, hah. Tell me, what camera are you using?"

I opened the case and put my camera on the counter. The eyes shone even more brightly, and another tear rolled down the same cheek.

"Dear me," Mr Rayne said happily. "A Zeiss Ikon. Wonderful lenses."

"It's the Super Ikonta II."

I knew I'd been right to come here by the way he opened the camera: he handled it as though he were Sir Galahad with the Holy Grail.

"A lovely machine," he said. "Not like the mass-produced, automated rubbish they make these days. Where did you get it?"

"It was my granddad's. He bought it in Germany when he was there with the army."

I allowed him another minute of nostalgia. In a way I feel the same about that old camera, but I wouldn't mind a Leica minimum auto SLR instead. One day I'll have both.

"Do you do developing?" I said.

"Eh? Well, not personally, except for myself, of course. I send it away. Works out cheaper. Takes about three days."

"What's the quality like?"

"Quite adequate for most people." Mr Rayne sounded defensive. Then he started getting angry – with the world, not with me: "It's all holiday snaps these days. Beastly little point-and-shoot cameras. No artistry. No technique. It was very different when I was a boy."

"Yeah." I put the double-exposed film on the counter. "Is there an express service?"

"I'm afraid not." He looked at the film and then back at the camera. "Black and white, eh?"

"Double-exposed," I said. "I'm trying a sort of dream sequence."

"Ah – and you're in a hurry?"

"We're here on holiday," I explained. "I suppose I could take it back with me and do it at home."

His face puckered. "Unwise to leave exposed film hanging around. You never know what might happen to it."

I nodded sadly and waited.

"Tell you what," he went on. "I'll make an exception and do it myself. Always a pleasure to help a fellow enthusiast."

Once he'd made up his mind to help, there was no stopping him. He'd do me a set of prints for the price of a contact print. ("You can't even begin to judge a photo-graph by a contact print.") He'd have them ready by the end of the afternoon.

I looked at Smith.

"It depends on Frances," she said. "She's the one with transport. You might have to wait till tomorrow morning."

The bell clanked behind me as a man came into the shop.

"Morning, Jim," said Mr Rayne, looking more harassed than ever, "Won't be a minute. I've got the weddings for you. And the dog show will be ready this afternoon, I promise you."

"The editor's going to crucify me if it isn't. His wife's on the breeders' committee."

"Mr Hingham," Mr Rayne explained to Smith and me, "works for our local paper."

"We've all got to make a living," Hingham said. He had slanting brown eyes and very yellow teeth, like a dog's. "Look, Ron, I'm in a rush. I'll come in this afternoon."

"I'd better have your address," Mr Rayne said to me. "Just in case there's a hitch."

I glanced at Smith, who shrugged and said: "Youlgreave Mill, Quanton St John, I guess."

Hingham paused in the doorway. "That cottage near Youlgreave Barton? You'd better watch out. They say the ghost is walking again."

The bell clanked again, and he was gone.

"I knew it," Smith said. "That place is haunted. Sometimes I think I might be psychic."

"You didn't believe him? He was just having us on. Old Rayne didn't know anything about a ghost."

"Yeah but he wouldn't, necessarily. All he's interested in is photography. He didn't even know where Youlgreave Barton is."

I poured myself a second cup of proper tea. We were in a little café on the High Street, killing time before we were due to meet Frances. This ghost business was really getting up my nose. I mean, how gullible can you get? Smith was the last person I'd have expected to be superstitious.

She sipped her Coke. "Hingham's a newspaperman," she said slowly. "It's his job to hear things like that."

"Give it a break."

"You got to keep an open mind, Chris."

"Oh, sure," I said, wondering if country life was infecting Smith's brain. I made a big effort and decided against asking her if she still had an open mind about

32

Santa Claus and the Tooth Fairy. The prospect of seeing Frances again wasn't bringing out the nicer side of my nature.

The conversation died on us. Soon after that we left, because Smith wanted to buy a bottle of shampoo and some make-up on the way back to the car. That was a bad move. Frances sailed into the chemist's and trapped us by the cosmetics counter.

Frances stared out of the window while she was waiting to be served.

"I don't believe it," she said to us. "There's yet another ageing hippie. One just can't get away from them here."

It was the man with the torn yellow tee-shirt and long red hair tied back in a pony tail. An hour before, Frances had been shaking hands with him.

"And now," Frances said after lunch, "We've got the whole afternoon in front of us. How shall we fill it?"

Neither of us said anything. You know, I felt almost sorry for her. I suddenly realized that it couldn't be much fun for her to have us two tagging along. We didn't share her tastes. Smith was downright rude to her most of the time. Drew, the person she was meant to be having a holiday with, was wrapped up in his report, leaving his daughter and daughter's friend to her. If I'd been Frances, I'd have been feeling that Drew was bucking his responsibilities.

"We could have a walk along Offa's Dyke," she went on. "Or there's a Dutch water garden that's open to the public. Or – "

"You want to take some photographs of the village," Smith said, "Don't you, Chris?"

I nodded. I would have agreed to anything that prevented Frances from organizing us. That was her real problem, I decided, this need to tell people what to do. She was in the wrong job. She'd have made a great sergeant major.

Frances looked relieved. "Well, if that's what you really *want*," she said. "I'd rather like to have a look at the church here."

We were sitting in the garden of the Youlgreave Arms in Quanton St John. Once again we had time to kill. Drew wasn't expecting us at the Mill until four o'clock.

"I don't think I want to stay here much longer," Frances said. "It's abominably noisy."

For once she had a point. The place was crowded. Each pair of adults in the garden seemed to be attached to at least three children. All the children were under school age, and most of them were trying to get on the slide at once. Either that or they were falling off the swing or trying to drown themselves in the pond.

"Why can't their parents control them?" Frances said angrily.

"They weren't like that in our day," said a podgy little man at the next table. "Were they, love?"

It took Frances a moment to work out that he was talking to her. Then her eyes flicked across to the man and the woman who was with him. The bloke looked like he'd booked the wrong holiday – he was dressed for the Costa del Something: a sort of package-holiday jetsetter, complete with gold chains and a little handbag. The woman was the female equivalent. I'd noticed earlier that she'd kicked off her stiletto-heeled shoes under the table. They were both on their second bottle of extra-strong lager.

"No, indeed," Frances said haughtily. She turned back to us. "Now we really must be going."

"Going to see the church?" the man said. "Beautiful, isn't it?"

"Like something on a calendar," the woman chipped in.

"Well, goodbye," Frances said firmly. She stuck her nose in the air and herded us out of the garden.

"I do loathe people who try to strike up conversations with perfect strangers," she said.

"Seems a pretty harmless activity to me," Smith said. "I guess we'll see you back at the car."

Frances went off to the church and we sauntered away in the opposite direction. I waited until she was out of earshot.

"That red-haired hippie outside the chemist's," I said. "He was the one she was shaking hands with."

"You're imagining it. Not the hippie, I mean, but seeing them shaking hands."

"I'm not. I – "

"Maybe you made a mistake. You only saw them for a split second. It might have just looked as if they were shaking hands."

I said nothing. The trouble with Smith and me, I thought, is that we're both obstinate: she's got her ghost and I've got the hippie. And we were both in foul moods to begin with. We had another one of those silences that reminded me of the first time we met, when she had a tendency to treat me like something grey and slimy she'd found under a stone.

Quanton St John had looked on the dull side when we drove through it yesterday. It didn't take me long to realize that I'd made a mistake: in fact it was dead boring. The village had one street. Most of the road was lined with these twee little cottages that looked like a collective advertisement for a pension scheme. In a couple of minutes we reached the new housing estate, where houses with cramped gardens huddled together for protection in a sort of executive ghetto.

Back we went, past the Youlgreave Arms. The jet-setter gave us a cheery wave. He was on his third bottle of lager and had taken off his shirt. We inspected the one shop, which was closed. I wondered what the locals did on Saturday nights. Tell each other ghost stories round the fire?

At the far end of the village was the church and the graveyard around it. The church meant Frances so that was out. Anyway, I like cemeteries.

"You haven't taken any photos," Smith said.

"It's all too pretty. But maybe I can find a photogenic gravestone."

"Kind of morbid, isn't it?"

On the other side of the churchyard, we came across a plain stone marker, smeared with yellowy-green lichen that was almost fluorescent. The inscription said: "J.B.

36

1719". Best of all, someone had balanced an empty beer can on the top of the stone.

"One for the road," I said, opening the camera case.

Smith looked blankly at me, then laughed.

It took a while to set up the shot. In the end I lay on my stomach so I could tilt the camera up at the grave-stone. Maybe it wouldn't work. Maybe it would only appeal to someone with my sense of humour. Smith sat in the sun with her back against another gravestone and shut her eyes.

I took the picture and then swung the camera on Smith. God, what a cliché: the sleeping beauty. It's funny how all the expression and half the individuality are lost from a face when the eyes are closed. Just before I pressed the shutter she opened her eyes.

"You – " Then her face changed. "We've got visitors."

I turned round. Mr and Mrs Jet-Setter were struggling towards us. He was sweating, and his face glowed like a lightbulb. She was limping along on the high heels, trying to light a cigarette as she walked.

"Hi, there," said the man, panting. He gave me a man-to-man leer. He was adding up me and Smith and the beer can, and getting the wrong answer. "Having a spot of rest and recreation, eh?"

"Brian, have you got a match? My lighter's packed up."

Brian ignored her. "I don't suppose you've seen a friend of ours around? A black girl, in her twenties. I know she's on holiday somewhere around here, and we were hoping to run into her."

Two things hit me at the same time. First, I hadn't seen *anyone* with a black skin since I got to this part of the world. It was as if I'd travelled from London to another country. Second, Brian's question had an urgency about it that didn't fit with what he'd actually said.

Smith said, "No," though the question had been aimed at me.

"That's a shame," Brian said. "She works with Sammy

Jo here, you see. And it's her birthday on Thursday and we were hoping – "

"Why don't you ask *him*?" Smith pointed down the path behind them. It was a fairly polite way of saying "Go away".

A middle-aged man was coming towards us. Everything about him was grey and boring: he looked like a bank clerk. His face was long with disapproval, and he had his eye on the beer can. Oh God, I thought. Probably a beer can on a gravestone counted as heresy or blasphemy or something.

"I should tell you," he said in a tired voice. "We don't really like drinking in the churchyard. Or litter, for that matter."

"Don't worry," Smith said. "We didn't put it there, and we'll find a trash can for it when we go."

He gave her a smile that made him seem almost human. "Don't think I'm being officious. I'm a churchwarden here, you see, and the rector and everyone else tend to hold me personally responsible for every blade of grass."

If the rector was Mr Gisburn, the bloke didn't have an easy job to do. Sammy Jo was hiding her unlit cigarette behind her back, like a guilty school girl. Brian coughed and said he thought they might as well be getting along.

"Aren't you going to ask him about your friend?" Smith said.

Brian shuffled his feet and explained.

The churchwarden shook his head. "I haven't seen her – black people stand out around here." The smile briefly reappeared. "Of course we used to have a black woman in the village – "

"Eh?" Brian interrupted. "When was that?"

"Nearly three hundred years ago." The churchwarden nodded towards J.B.'s gravestone. "In a sense she's never left."

It should have been funny but the hairs rose on the

38

back of my arm. Don't ask me why. Smith is the one who's meant to be psychic.

Brian grunted. "Yeah, well never mind. Come on, Sammy Jo."

He grabbed her arm and practically dragged her away.

The churchwarden stared thoughtfully after them.

"A black woman?" Smith said. "That was unusual, wasn't it?"

"Less so than you might think. The slave trade was big business in those days. Some of the gentry liked to have a black slave on the premises. One up on the neighbours."

"A sort of status symbol, you mean?"

"Yes. Nowadays, I suppose, it'd be a jacuzzi or an Irish wolfhound. We've become a bit more civilized. Our local family, the Youlgreaves, had two black slaves – twins. That must have really put the neighbours' noses out of joint."

"The Youlgreaves?" Smith sounded hoarse. "They lived at Youlgreave Barton?"

The man nodded, surprised. "You know it?"

"We're staying at the Mill."

"Ah, I see." He hesitated, his face suddenly blank. "Well, you mustn't let me bore you. Local history is something of a hobby of mine. If you want to know more, there's a section on the Youlgreaves in the church guide." He coughed modestly. "As a matter of fact I wrote it. Er – I hope you have a good holiday."

The smile reappeared for an instant. Then he ambled away.

Smith said, "Come on. I want to buy that guide."

"Frances is in the church. Remember?"

"You can stay here if you want," she said, picking up the beer can.

We went down to the gate, where there was a litter bin, and then up to the church. To my surprise, Frances wasn't inside – not unless she was lurking behind a pillar or under a pew. There was a table by the door with post-cards, a pile of guides and the usual religious leaflets you see in a church. The guide cost 50p. *A Short History of the Church and Village of Quanton St John* by T.W. Anthorn. Smith stuffed a £1 coin in the box, which seemed a bit over the top to me. I bought a postcard to send my parents. On the way out Smith pointed at a marble plaque on the wall. I looked at it and wished she hadn't seen it.

It had an urn at the top with a woman in flowing clothes propped up against it. Below was carved in old-fashioned writing:

Near this place are deposited the Remains
of
JAMES HENRY YOULGREAVE
Only Son of Charles Youlgreave, Esq., and
Henrietta his Wife, Who was Foully Murth-
ered by a Savage Ingrate on July 29th, 1719,
in the 21st year of his Life. His Courteous
Disposition, his Excellent Understanding
and most Christian Temper rendered him
universally belov'd while living and
lamented when dead. Mourning their
untimely Loss, his sorrowing Parents and
Sister . . .

There was a good deal more, mainly about the dead man's hopes of Eternal Bliss.

"You see the date," Smith said. "1719 – same as J.B. Do you think there's a connection?"

"No," I said sourly. "Why should there be?"

We trailed back to J.B.'s gravestone. Quite a contrast. Youlgreave had a prominent position in the church, out of the weather, and that chatty little character reference to the Almighty, all tastefully presented in marble: no expense spared. Poor old J.B. had nothing but her initials and the date.

Smith sat down to read the guide. I thought I might as well do the card to my parents. I wrote their address and spent the next ten minutes chewing the end of the pen and wondering what to write next. The things that were on my mind were not the sort of things you can tell your parents; not that I wanted to in any case. In the end I wrote: *Weather sunny. See you Saturday. Chris.*

"Chris," Smith said. She sounded breathless.

I looked up. Her eyes were bright with tears.

"That Goddamn man," she said. Smith hardly swears at all, unlike most people I know. "The creep. The dirty little schmuck. I'd like to strangle him. Slowly."

"Who are we talking about?"

"James Henry, of course. Do you know what he did? They had these two slaves as sort of household pets. Called them John and Jenny Black and made them wear silver collars round their necks. James Henry sort of owned John, and his sister had Jenny. They grew up together, right? Almost like siblings. Then good old James seduced Jenny and got her pregnant; more likely he raped her. John protested and James got out the horsewhip. Quaint old rural custom for handling slave relations. And there was a fight, and John killed him, probably in self-defence."

She bit her lip and looked down at the guide.

"The 'Savage Ingrate'?" I said.

Smith said, "They got out the hounds and hunted him across country. Then they hung him. Jenny was in the same room while they were fighting. James hit her with the whip. She had a miscarriage. And died."

I looked at the little gravestone. I'd like to say I was thinking of nothing but the 300-year-old tragedy. It was more complicated than that. I was wondering why Smith was so upset by it, and whether there was something wrong with me because I didn't feel the same. And another part of me was wondering what would happen if I put my arm round Smith's shoulders. After all, it's what you do when people are upset.

She stood up suddenly. I'd missed my chance.

"Where you going?" I said.

"There's something I want to ask Anthorn – where it all happened. Are you coming?"

Anthorn was down by the gate. He wasn't alone. Frances had appeared from somewhere and was chatting to him and Gisburn the Rabid Rector. I told Smith I'd wait.

I filled in time by taking a photograph of the church tower. I had one simple ambition: to make it look like anything *but* a church tower. And all the time I was thinking about how nearly I put my arm around Smith, and how she was thinking so much about ghosts and Youlgreaves that she had no room in her head for me. Pathetic.

She came back in about five minutes.

"It did happen at Youlgreave Barton."

"Uh huh," I said. "You do surprise me."

Then she did surprise me.

"Anthorn's got to go into town to pick up something from his office. He's offered to take us if you want. I thought maybe you'd like to pick up those photographs. Frances says it's okay."

Anthorn drove us back to town. On the way Smith kept him talking about the Youlgreaves.

"The ghost?" he said. "No, it's not either of the men. It's meant to be Jenny. I've never seen it."

Anthorn was a bit like a ghost himself – thin and grey and dried-out. I imagined him spending his working life counting endless £5 notes. I'd rather shoot myself.

"We met this guy at Mr Rayne's," Smith said. "Some kind of reporter."

"His name was Jim Hingham," I said, just to prove I was part of this conversation too.

"Oh, I know him," Anthorn said.

"He said the ghost was walking again."

"Well, he would," Anthorn said. "Anything to encourage a good story. That's his job. If he mentions the ghost of Jenny to enough people, sooner or later one of them will think they've seen it. It's human nature."

When we reached the town, Anthorn glanced at me. "Do you mind if I collect my stuff first?"

"Sure," I said.

"Then I'll drive you on to Ronald Rayne's. I want to do a bit of shopping in the same street."

Anthorn indicated left and braked. I congratulated myself: Barclays Bank was just coming up. Instead he turned into the car park of the police station beyond the bank. He reversed rapidly into a slot near a side door.

"Won't be long." He got out of the car, leaving the keys in the ignition.

Smith and I looked at each other.

"Did *you* know we were coming here?" I said.

She shook her head.

Anthorn went into the building. I got out of the car and walked to the back. All these parking slots had little plates screwed to the wall behind them.

The one behind our car said: *Detective Inspector T. W. Anthorn*.

CHAPTER FIVE

"Well, he's got to do something for a living," Smith said fifteen minutes later. "So he's a cop. What's the big deal?"

The word police meant different things to her and me. It was too complicated to explain so I took out my diary. I keep addresses and phone numbers in the back.

"I'm going to ring Clive," I said. "He might have some news about the tickets."

"I'll stay here."

Smith was giving nothing away: I still didn't know if she really wanted to see Paul Anders or not.

We'd already been to Rayne's and picked up the prints, which were so awful I couldn't believe it. Now we were waiting for Anthorn on the green by the Abbey. There was a phone box on the corner.

The phone rang and rang. At last there was a click and Clive's voice said, "Uh. Hullo. What time is it?"

"Nearly half-past four. And it's Tuesday afternoon."

"Is that Chris?" he said. "You woke me up."

"So I guessed. Rough night?"

He yawned. "I can't remember."

It has to be admitted that Clive is a little on the degenerate side. He's a good mechanic but he never holds down a job for long. It's always the same story: he just can't wake up on time more than three days running. His taste for clubs and all-night parties may have something to do with it.

"Listen," I said. "Did you get the tickets?"

"Paul Anders? Yeah, no problem. Hey, there's a new nightclub on the Fulham Road. I got a couple of complimentaries for the opening. Do you think you could find out if Judith would be interested? I tried phoning her but she wouldn't talk to me."

"Sure," I said. I knew what Judith's answer would be but there was no harm in trying. "I'm really grateful about those tickets. Look, if I come on Saturday, maybe with a friend, do you think we could sleep on your floor?"

"No problem." Clive yawned again. "But why Saturday? The tickets are for Wednesday."

"Wednesday?" I shouted. "You mean tomorrow?"

"It was Wednesday or nothing. The guy I got them from said – "

"Okay. I'll see if I can work something out."

I stared out of the phone box at Smith, who was sitting cross-legged on the grass outside. I'd already given Clive the money. If we couldn't make it, that was £15 up the spout. Wednesday or nothing: probably nothing.

"Did Judith get the roses I sent?"

"Yeah," I said. "You're in with a chance."

Anthorn was crossing the road with a carrier bag in each hand. Smith stood up.

"What did she say exactly?"

Judith's exact words had been: "I wonder where he nicked *those* from."

Aloud I said: "Sorry, Clive – I got to go. I'll be in touch."

I was relieved to have the excuse. Once Clive starts asking about Judith, it's almost impossible to make him stop.

Anthorn dropped us at the end of the lane. As Smith and I were walking up to the Mill, I told her what Clive had said.

She shook her head, as I'd guessed she would. "Sorry. I can't make it that soon. But maybe you could go. Isn't there someone else you could go with?"

"I'll see him next time round."

No one else I knew was into Paul Anders. In any case I

45

didn't want to go with someone else or even by myself: I wanted to go with Smith.

"Have you paid for the tickets?" she said.

"Yes. But probably Clive can find a buyer for them."

That was bending the truth. It was a miracle that Clive had got himself sufficiently organized to buy them in the first place. A second miracle would be too much to hope for. Mentally I kissed goodbye to £15. It wasn't a nice feeling. Nor was missing Paul Anders.

"If he doesn't manage to sell them," Smith said, "maybe I could sort of – "

"No," I said. I wasn't taking her money.

She sneaked a look at my face and changed the subject. If she'd been a gearbox, she'd have made a loud grating noise.

"I'd like to see those prints when we get back." And she went on to ask a whole lot of questions about photography. I knew she was trying to make up for not wanting to go to the concert. But sometimes an attempt to be tactful and sympathetic is like using an electric sander on an open wound.

Drew and Frances were sitting on deckchairs in the yard. They were celebrating with a pot of Lapsang Souchong the fact that Drew had finished his report ahead of time.

"I'm going to fax it off to my secretary," he said. "Frances says the bookstore in town has a fax machine. Then we can start enjoying ourselves."

"You'll have some tea," Frances told us.

I could hardly throw mine in the stream in front of her. To my surprise I quite enjoyed it. I suppose you get used to anything in time, if you're thirsty enough.

"Well, what have you been doing then?" Drew asked.

He really seemed to want to know. He was like a different person – cracking jokes and generally being the life and soul of the party. Smith blossomed under the attention he gave her. Maybe, I thought, just maybe the rest of the week isn't going to be as bad as the first 24 hours. Two seconds later I changed my mind.

"Frances and I are planning going out to dinner tonight," Drew said. "A sort of celebration. Do you guys want to come?"

Smith glanced at Frances and then at me. She wasn't looking so happy now. "We could fix ourselves something here. We haven't listened to those tapes yet. What do you think, Chris?"

I nodded. I guessed she didn't want to play gooseberry with her dad and Frances. Romantic candlelit dinners aren't so romantic when there's more than two of you. I was relieved for my own sake. It would have meant two or three hours trapped round a table; like last night but worse. I'm no good at small talk, not with people like Drew and Frances.

"Right," Drew said cheerfully. "If that's the way you want it."

I saw Smith's face, just for one unguarded moment, and wished that Drew hadn't made it quite so obvious that that was the way he wanted it too.

He was looking at his watch, not her. "There's just enough time."

"For what?" Frances said.

"I could drive into town and get the report off now. You don't mind?"

"No, of course not – you'll feel happier once it's out of the way."

He fetched a folder and the car keys from the cottage. He kissed Frances on the cheek, smiled in the general direction of me and Smith, and drove off in the Peugeot. I shut the gate behind him to keep the cows at bay.

"So you got the photos," Frances said. "May I see them?"

I squirmed internally but gave them to her. The double-exposure experiment had been a failure, and I didn't want the results on public view. Besides, I didn't think Frances really wanted to see them: she was just being polite, if that's the word I want.

She skimmed through them at a speed that simultaneously irritated me and made me grateful. Then she launched into what sounded like an alarmingly well-informed lecture on the use of double exposure in the nineteenth century. Meanwhile Smith picked up the photos and went through them more slowly. I wanted to watch her but I had to look at Frances because she was talking to me (or rather *at* me). Out of the corner of my eye I saw that one of the prints was really interesting her. But Frances wouldn't stop talking.

"Listen," Smith said. "Sounds like a car coming up the lane."

This was quite an event for us Keystone Trusties so we all listened. A flashy little Escort XR3i – bright red and with about half a dozen aerials – drew up alongside the gate. Two people got out.

"Hi," Brian said, oozing matiness. "Hey, we've already met."

"At the pub, remember?" Sammy Jo chipped in, looking at Frances. "And we met your children up at the church."

Smith snorted. Sammy Jo stepped backwards and swore under her breath. She wasn't prepared for cow pats.

"Well, what a coincidence," Brian said. "This mill is such a fascinating relic of medieval industry. I hope it's okay, us turning up like this. We just couldn't resist coming to have a peep, could we, Sammy Jo?"

Sammy Jo, who was trying to scrape the cow pat off her shoe without being too obvious about it, said yes and tried to look enthusiastic.

"The Keystone Trust has done a marvellous job." Brian ran his eyes round the yard. "Just look at the quality of the repointing."

It was all wrong. Brian and Sammy Jo weren't potential

Keystone Trusties. I looked forward to finding out how Frances would give them the elbow.

But Frances was smiling at them. "How nice to meet fellow enthusiasts," she said. "Would you like to have a look inside?" She added to Smith: "Get some cups, dear, and put the kettle on."

She whisked them into the house. The guided tour only took a couple of minutes. Brian said it had been a real privilege and yes they'd love some tea.

Smith brought out the cups and said to me, "Let's go see what food we've got."

She practically dragged me into the house.

"What's Frances up to?" I said when we reached the kitchen.

Smith shrugged.

I tried again. "Look, it doesn't make sense, does it? She treats them like pariahs in the pub, and now she can't do enough for them. And Brian's no more interested in architecture than I am. Why's she – ?"

"Did you bring the photos?" Smith interrupted.

"They're still outside. Why?"

She looked through the kitchen window. "We'll get them later. Listen, did you look at the last print?"

"Of course I did."

"Youlgreave Barton, right? The shot you took yesterday. And the other image was an upside-down tree."

I nodded. The tree was upside down because with my camera it had been easier to invert the roll of film between the first and second exposures, rather than wind it back on to its original spool. The last print was one of the worst of the batch: the branches on the tree were underexposed and therefore too dark; they wrecked the pattern of shadows and window frames on the wall of the house.

"Did you see it?" She was standing really close to me, almost touching. "The top window on the left?"

I sighed. "See what?"

"There's a black face on the other side of the glass. A woman."

"Smith," I said slowly. "Let's get this straight. Ghosts don't exist, only in people's heads. I didn't see a face there."

To be honest I'd hardly looked at the photograph. It was the last of the 16 prints. By the time I'd reached it, I'd had enough of my failures.

"It *was* there," Smith said, backing away from me. "In the lower left-hand corner. It wasn't very clear because of the glass."

"Then how did you know it was a woman?" I snapped.

"Because of the hair. You could see the shape."

"Watch out," I said, nodding towards the window.

Frances was on the move. She came into the kitchen for some milk. Brian or Sammy Jo had no qualms about polluting their Lapsang. It gave me a moment to think.

"Light and dark can play weird tricks sometimes, especially on a black-and-white print."

"It wasn't a trick of the light. I'm sure."

"And it was double exposed, remember. Maybe something on the first exposure sort of created the illusion – "

"Chris!" she yelled. "Will you listen to me? Just for a moment? It was a face. Not obvious but once you noticed it you couldn't mistake it."

I leant against the table. There were too many possibilities. Smith might be crazy, which I didn't think was true. She could be mistaken, but no one was going to convince her of that. Mr Rayne might have grafted the face on to my print, God knows why; but treble exposures are technically possible. Or the face really did belong to a ghost, which seemed unlikely – but I'm not an expert on everything the universe may or may not contain so I couldn't be absolutely, oath-on-the-Bible sure.

"What about the friend that Sammy Jo and Brian are looking for?" I said. "She's a black woman."

"You think she could get past Gisburn? Do you think

he'd give her a key? Do you think a friend of Sammy Jo's would want to see inside a place like that? Besides, you're forgetting the vibrations. Be reasonable."

Coming from her, the advice seemed a bit unfair. Whatever the truth, I knew one thing for certain: that Smith believed that a woman who'd died more than 300 years before had somehow appeared on that photograph.

"Okay," I said, wanting to let her down gently. "We'll have a proper look at the photo – and the negative. Maybe we should show them to your dad and Frances – "

"No, not Frances. Nor Dad, because he'd want to show her."

Smith was right. I could imagine Frances' reaction. Let's - try - and - play - along - with - the - children's - little - game. Even the idea made me cringe.

"Someone objective," Smith went on. "How about that guy Anthorn? He knows the background."

"All right." I was secretly relieved: you couldn't get much more down-to-earth than a cop.

"And maybe . . ." Smith hesitated. "Well, if it is the ghost, you could even make some money. I bet Hingham would pay for a photo of it."

I knew she didn't want me to sell her ghost to Hingham or anyone else. Outside there was a roar from the Escort's engine.

"Let's think about that one," I said. "Maybe it's not such a good idea."

Smith smiled at me. Our eyes locked together, or that's how it felt to me. Then Frances came in with the tea tray.

"Have you sorted out your meal yet?" she said.

"We were just going to," Smith said.

Frances was delighted. "I'll see what I can find."

"Great. Chris and I'll be right back."

We bolted outside. The prints were still on the wall by the stream, spread out beside the cardboard wallet they came in. Smith leafed through them.

"Chris, it's not here. You have a look."

I took the prints and dealt them one by one on to the wall, counting as I went. 15 prints. There should have been 16. The one of Youlgreave Barton had gone.

Smith dropped the wallet on the wall. She said in a despairing voice: "What do you know? They've taken the negatives too."

CHAPTER SIX

"I thought they'd never go," Smith said. "And what did you think of her clothes? That red dress makes her look like a stuffed tomato."

Tactfully I said nothing. Frances had dressed to kill. Drew was practically panting for the slaughterhouse.

We listened to the Peugeot's engine diminishing in volume. Frances changed down for the junction with the B road. Then silence. The dreadful, yawning silence of a country evening.

It was still light. Behind us was the ridge of Oscar's Castle. Two people were walking along the top. Hippies probably: they were so far away they looked like animated matchstick men. Drew and Frances wouldn't be back for at least three or four hours.

Smith grunted angrily. She went into the kitchen and came back with a can of beer and two glasses. We sat down on the wall.

"Item one," she said, opening the beer, "the Rabid Rector."

"He could be just naturally rabid. A coincidence."

"Okay, we'll put him on hold. Number two's the atmosphere at Youlgreave Barton."

"Feeling," I said. "Not fact."

"*I* felt it. Fact. Three: Frances and her moonlit walk, which might be totally innocent. Four: the hippie she pretended she didn't know. According to you."

"Fact. I saw them shaking hands."

Smith handed me a glass. "In that case the ghost in the window counts as fact. I saw that. What number's that?"

"Five. Do we need all these numbers?"

"It pays to be rational about this," she said. "Six is

Brian and Sammy Jo turning up and pretending to be Keystone Trusties. Seven is Frances pretending to believe them."

"And eight, someone nicks the photo and the negative."

"Has to be either Frances or Brian and Sammy Jo."

"None of it makes sense," I said. "And what about your dad?"

"If she's up to something, he's so besotted with her he wouldn't notice. Sometimes he can be so *stupid*."

That made a sort of sense. We sat sipping beer. The ridge was empty now. I thought of two things Smith might want to do, and neither of them had the least attraction for me. I wanted to sit with Smith on this wall and drink beer.

"I think," Smith said in a muffled voice, "he's going to end up marrying her. I've never seen him like this before. He's serious."

"He wouldn't marry her if he found out she'd been stringing him along. Making a fool of him somehow."

Smith looked at me over the edge of her glass. "We could search her bags."

That was the lesser of the two evils I'd dreamed up.

"Okay," I said. "If you want."

"I don't *want* to." She sounded angry, with herself. "But it might help us get a handle on this."

So we finished the beer and went upstairs to the bedroom Frances shared with Drew. We went through everything – her bags, her clothes, an astonishing number of books, her make-up, even the postcards she'd written and stamped. We were very thorough, and very careful not to disturb anything. And we found nothing that was even slightly incriminating.

"This is dumb," Smith said viciously.

As we left she banged the bedroom door. She fetched another can from the fridge and we went back to the wall.

"Now what?" she said. "There must be something we can do."

Maybe the beer loosened my tongue. Maybe I'm just stupid.

"I suppose we could take a look at Youlgreave Barton."

"You mean take a look inside?"

That hadn't been what I meant. I'd been thinking of a stroll round the garden, which was bad enough. Smith was looking at me, and I fooled myself that I saw admiration in her eyes. The prospect of breaking into Youlgreave Barton scared the hell out of me.

"Of course," I said. "What else?"

As the light faded, I liked the idea less and less.

Frances had left a big car torch in the sitting room. Smith slung it over her shoulder and went into the kitchen. When she came out she was holding a couple of knives.

"Oh, I get it," I said. "You can make a cricifix with the knives. Shouldn't we get some garlic too?"

She ignored that. "What about your camera?"

"No point. I haven't got flash."

"Can you think of anything else to take?"

"God, I don't know. I've never been ghost-busting before. The Dynamic Duo investigate the haunted manor. All we need's a faithful dog. You tie a message round his collar and he charges off and fetches Scotland Yard."

"You don't have to come," she said. "Put your feet up. Have another beer. Listen to Paul Anders."

"I'm coming," I said. "Just getting myself into the mood."

We turned out the lights and went outside. Smith locked the door. I moved towards the gate.

"Hush," she whispered. "Someone's there."

There were footsteps coming along the lane from the direction of Youlgreave Barton. One person doing a quick

55

march in heavy boots. Tramp, tramp, tramp: someone who didn't give a damn about the cow pats.

We crouched in the shelter of the hedge by the gate. At this stage we weren't even doing anything wrong but that wasn't how it felt. A moment later the Reverend Mr Gisburn pounded past the gate. He was muttering to himself and carrying his stick like a rifle on his shoulder.

"What's he up to?" Smith murmured in my ear.

I shrugged. "The main thing is, he's not at Youlgreave Barton. If we'd been five minutes earlier, we'd have run slap into him."

When everything was quiet again we set off. It was twilight now – not exactly dark but the shadows were gathering. I was glad that Smith hadn't decided to wait till midnight in the interests of psychic research.

All too soon we reached the iron gate with the TRES-PASSERS WILL BE PROSECUTED notice. Smith climbed over first and took a few steps towards the house. She stopped and waited for me to catch up with her.

Suddenly every movement we made seemed twice as loud. The shadows circled a little closer to us, like Red Indians round the wagon train. I had the strangest feeling this had all happened before. Then I remembered. Once I had a dream in which I walked into a living room. It was empty and brightly lit, except for the fact that one wall was a sheet of darkness. And in the dream I suddenly realized that I'd walked on to a stage, and on the other side of that non-existent wall was an audience of thousands, watching me. That was when the dream became a nightmare.

"Right," I said – a little more forcefully than I'd intended. "Let's walk round the house."

We struggled through the ruined garden to the place where I'd taken the photograph. On the way we examined all the ground-floor windows. Only the big window at the end was covered with corrugated iron. On the others, sheets of plywood had been cut to size and nailed to the frames.

"That's new," I said.

"How do you know?"

"The heads of the nails haven't rusted yet. And the wood's not even begun to discolour."

Round the corner was a wall pierced by a small archway that had once been filled by a gate. Gisburn must have come through there when he surprised us yesterday.

On the other side of the wall was a rutted yard. I bashed my shin against a Ford Anglia that had been left to rot just inside the gateway: it had no wheels and windows, and it was so rusty that you couldn't tell what its original colour had been. On our right was what looked like the back of the house; on the left was a range of barns and stables. They were much younger than the house and in even worse condition.

"Here's the door that Gisburn uses," Smith said.

She was peering into a porch. It was so gloomy in there that I shone the torch on it. The door was a dead ringer for the one at the Mill – just as old and just as strong. The only difference was that this one had a new brass padlock on it.

"It's like a fortress," I said. "We're not going to be able to get in. Not with a couple of knives."

I must have sounded too cheerful because Smith rounded on me.

"You chickening out or something? Don't mind me. I'll go on by myself."

"I'm just stating facts," I snapped. "Someone's made this place as tight as a drum."

"We're only halfway round."

"Sure," I said, "and we'll check the other half. I wouldn't miss it for the world."

She started to say something, turned away and then stopped. "You know why we're doing this?" she said. "Scrapping like a pair of kids? We're scared, Chris. It's the vibrations. What happened here left a sort of imprint on the place. You can't pretend you don't feel it."

"I don't have to pretend. This is just an empty house, okay? Let's get it over with. I'm hungry."

The twilight was deepening. In half an hour it would be dark. I wasn't frightened – just uneasy; but I was damned if I'd admit it to Smith. So I pushed through the sea of waist-high weeds and forced my way into a walled enclosure that had once had a roof on it. I scrambled up to a window opening without any glass and wriggled through it. The rest of the house and garden were on the other side.

If the house was T-shaped, this front was the top of the crossbar. And it looked as if once upon a time the house had been shaped like a cross. Two triangles of masonry, like crumbling stone staircases, marked the point where another wing had been tacked on to the building. It must have fallen down a long time before because windows had been inserted in the wall between the buttresses.

The lower windows were boarded up. One of the upper ones, a sash window, was open a few inches. The edge of the frame was no more than a foot away from the nearest buttress.

A stone staircase? Hell, I wasn't risking my neck on that, not for a ghost. There was a thud behind me as Smith jumped down. I turned back to her.

"Same old story," I said. "We'd need a crowbar or a sledgehammer to get inside."

She didn't take my word for it but checked the ground-floor windows one by one.

"Hey," I said, hoping to distract her attention. "That must be Oscar's Castle over there."

"Chris, come look at this."

She was standing at the foot of the buttress, staring at the open window. "Just like a staircase, huh?"

I decided to make the best of a bad business. "Looks like that window's open a crack."

Smith didn't wait to discuss it. She climbed up the buttress as coolly as if it had been a stepladder. And of course I had to follow. Her feet above me dislodged pockets of dirt and stone dust, which showered on to my face. Halfway up, a small tree had rooted itself into the stonework. I nearly fell off as I was working my way round it. The light was draining away like water out of a bath. It was sheer lunacy. And all the time Smith was whistling tunelessly through her teeth. I think she was actually enjoying it.

Finally we got there. Smith, still whistling, leant across to the window. "Easy," she said. "There's a sort of ledge under the windowsill."

I opened my eyes. Oh my God. She wasn't even on the buttress. She was clinging to the side of the wall: her feet in a hole where a stone had fallen out, one hand hooked over the sill and the other trying to force up the lower half of the window. I shut my eyes and wondered how I'd tell Drew that his daughter was lying with a broken back in the garden of Youlgreave Barton.

There was a sudden, inhuman screech.

So sudden and so inhuman that I made a sound that was the next best thing to a whimper. I opened my eyes in time to see Smith's legs disappearing into the house.

Then she was looking at me through the 18-inch gap between window and sill, her face a pale blur against the darkness of the room behind her.

"You coming? Or do you want to stay there?"

She held out her hand to help me, which made me ashamed. An even more powerful reason to get through the window was the thought of trying to get down that buttress in the dark. Once inside the house, I thought, there must be a way out – on the ground floor.

I took her hand and made a grab for the sill. My feet scrabbled against the wall for a few sickening seconds before I found the ledge. After that it was just a matter of a few more seconds of frantic wriggling between life and death. The next thing I knew I was huddled in the angle between wall and floor, just inside the window.

Smith, who apparently had no idea what was going on in my head, flashed the torch round the room. The plaster was falling off the walls, there was a hole in the floorboards near the open door and, directly over my head where the ceiling was meant to be, I saw a couple of stars twinkling in the sky.

"Someone's been here. Take a look."

She was poking a pile of rubbish in the fireplace. A weird mixture of things: an empty jar of peanut butter; a crumpled tissue; a Coke can; half a dozen used matches.

"It doesn't necessarily mean anything," I said. "Could have been there for years."

"No dust. This is recent."

"Well, maybe tramps were using the place, and that's why they had it boarded up. Not a ghost, anyway. They don't like peanut butter."

That earned one of her less friendly looks. Smith said she was going to search the place. I said okay but watch out for dry rot, wet rot, woodworm and deathwatch beetles. I also suggested we started with downstairs: I wanted to find a way out as soon as possible.

The first thing we saw on the landing was a dead rat. It hadn't been there very long: it looked as though it had settled down for a nap. Smith grabbed my hand and edged round the furry corpse to the head of the stairs.

It was a wooden staircase with carvings of fruit all over the place. It was also a deathtrap. One of the treads disintegrated as I put my foot on it. We got downstairs in one piece, but only just.

We went into the first room we came to. It was huge and ankle-deep with dust. There were two boarded-up windows at the far end. Most of the glass was broken. Something scuttered away in the corner and Smith moaned softly. A cobweb as thick as a handkerchief wrapped itself round my face. Then we abruptly forgot about the lack of mod cons.

There was a wrenching, tearing sound at the end of the room. Wood splintered. A current of air made the dust ripple like water beneath the lefthand window.

Smith snapped off the torch.

Someone else had come to Youlgreave Barton, and they'd come better prepared than us. They'd brought a crowbar.

The air was like a dark, clammy fog. It had got inside my head. I couldn't think. I couldn't move.

Smith's fingernails were digging into my arm. The pain gave me something to focus on. I realized she was trying to drag me away. She towed me out of the room, back to the foot of the stairs.

The door was still open but we could no longer see the window. Someone grunted. A whole panel of plywood gave way. The remains of the daylight seeped in. Torchlight spilled across the floor, through the doorway and into the hall. There was a crash and glass tinkled on to the floor.

My mind juddered into action again, and I wished it hadn't. We were in a stone prison with walls that were four-feet thick. We couldn't use the torch for fear of giving ourselves away. We didn't know the layout. If the condition of the stairs was anything to go by, the interior of Youlgreave Barton was a series of booby-traps.

"We got to get upstairs," Smith hissed.

"Too noisy."

Even if we got to the top without breaking any bones and safely out of the window, they'd catch us on the buttress. Anyway it was too late. Much too late.

Footsteps were crossing the room towards the door. The torchlight grew stronger. I saw the dim outlines of a doorway beside us. I pulled Smith inside. We made very little noise on the stone floor.

I didn't have a plan, only a prayer: I hoped the newcomer would go somewhere else, giving us time to make a bolt for the window he'd come in by.

"Ugh! It's like a bloody morgue in here. If you think I'm coming with you, you can think again."

The whispering voice was a woman's. It took me a second to realize it belonged to Sammy Jo.

"Shut up, will you?' Brian snapped. He was the one near the door and I don't think he was exactly cool, calm and collected either.

"No one would stay here," Sammy Jo said. "Not unless they were stark, staring mad."

"Just wait there."

"Don't leave me alone, Brian. Can't we just *say* we searched the place? I mean, who's to know? It's obvious no one's been here for centuries."

"Listen – we don't have a choice. He pays well but, let's face it, he's not got a nice nature. And he is not going to be pleased if he doesn't get his hands on that bloody woman. She's not at the Mill, is she? There's nowhere else to look."

For a few seconds he stood in the hall, flashing the torch this way and that. Then our door swung open and the light panned across the room. I swear I stopped breathing.

The light moved away and so did Brian's footsteps. He was checking out the ground floor as quickly as possible. He came back to the room where Sammy Jo was.

"If she's anywhere, she has to be upstairs," he whispered. "Someone's been here – there are marks in the dust all over the place."

"What if she's not?"

"Then we search the place properly. It's like a bloody maze."

Brian climbed the stairs, which wasn't as easy as he thought it would be. There was a cracking of rotten wood and a lot of swearing. It struck me that Brian and Sammy Jo weren't going about this very intelligently. If there were a woman here, she must have heard them breaking and entering.

"Now or never," Smith murmured.

She was right: it was brute force or nothing. Only Sammy Jo was between us and freedom. If she saw our faces, that was just too bad.

I followed her into the hall. There was a crash from upstairs: I think Brian had found a hole in the floor. His language got really obscene.

Smith charged into the room next door. She switched on the torch as she ran. I saw one of the knives glinting in her hand.

Sammy Jo was outside the window, leaning on the sill. She screamed.

I don't know which came first. The knowledge we'd miscalculated. The glimpse of what was in her hand. The shattering impact as the stone-flagged floor rose up and hit my body.

Or the sound of the shot.

The trouble with brute force is that other people have got either the will or the means to be more brutal than you have.

How were we to know that she'd have a gun? You just don't expect it. Not in England. And not in the hand of an overweight, slightly tarty woman like Sammy Jo. She'd seemed so *ordinary*.

"Bri!" Sammy Jo screeched over and over again. "Bri!"

Smith had hit the deck too. We lay there. The stone was cold against my cheek. Brian came down. He was waving an automatic.

"The kids from the Mill," Sammy Jo said in a voice that wobbled.

"You trying to wake the whole neighbourhood?" He wasn't bothered that someone might have got hurt.

"It just went off," she whined. "Anyway, there aren't any neighbours."

"Don't wave that gun at me," Brian yelled.

"Sorry. Bri, that girl's got a knife."

64

"Just stay by the window. Point the gun at them, not me, okay?"

Brian searched us. He found both knives. Then he prodded my leg with the toe of his shoe.

"Where is she? Don't muck me about."

"Who?"

That earned a kick. "We haven't got all night."

"Look, I don't know what you mean."

"Then what are you doing here?"

"Looking for ghosts," I said. "This is meant to be a haunted house."

"I knew it, Brian," Sammy Jo moaned. "I just knew it."

"Where are your parents?"

I nearly said "London" but that would have made things too complicated for Brian and possibly too painful for me.

"They went out to dinner," Smith said.

"The car was gone." Sammy Jo sounded peeved; maybe checking the Mill had been her responsibility. "No lights were on. Who'd have thought they'd leave these two behind?"

"You must have heard quite a lot," Brian said, giving me another prod with his foot.

"Not a thing, honest," I said rather too quickly. "We were up the other end of the house."

"How did you get in?"

"One of the upstairs windows."

Brian and Sammy Jo went into a huddle. It's amazingly unpleasant, I can tell you, trying without success to eavesdrop on a whispered conversation that concerns your future. But not as unpleasant as what happened next. Brian got Sammy Jo to come into the room. He left her standing over us while he went away – I assume to search the house more thoroughly. He was gone for what seemed like hours. We lay there, most of the time in silence, listening to him crashing about; you'd have thought he was trying to demolish the place.

Smith and I were lying facedown on the floor, which was strewn with dust and grit and probably rat-droppings. Worse of all was the thought of what might happen next. Sammy Jo kept muttering and moving around. At any moment her finger might have another little accident with the trigger.

When Brian came back he was in an even worse temper than before.

"Someone's been here," he said to Sammy Jo, without troubling to whisper. "I think we just missed her."

"So what do we do?"

He grunted. "Got no choice now, have we? Come on, kiddies, time for walkies."

"Can't we sort something out?" Smith said. "We won't mention this if you don't."

She might as well have saved her breath.

Sammy Jo was still looking at Brian. "This is going to cause problems, you know. You sure we should do this?"

"If you got a better idea, let's have it. This way at least we know what the risk is. And at least there's a chance of getting something out of it. But the other way – well, he's not the sort of bloke you take for a ride. I heard stories – "

"You never told me any of this."

"You didn't ask. Anyway, you were the one who liked the colour of his money."

"Is this a private quarrel?" Smith asked. "Or can anyone join in?"

They ran out of steam and just glared at Smith and then at one another. But they weren't really angry with each other. They were fighting for exactly the same reason as Smith and I had fought before we broke into this godawful place: because they were afraid.

We left Youlgreave Barton in convoy: Smith and me in front, with Sammy Jo and Brian immediately behind.

Every now and then Brian nudged my spine with the muzzle of his gun.

Outside it was almost completely dark. We stumbled through the garden and climbed over the gate. We went up the lane, away from the Mill.

I suppose in theory we could have made a break for it, perhaps in the garden. But two guns have a paralyzing effect on your powers of initiative. What really scared me was the memory of the shot that Sammy Jo had loosed off. Anyone, even Brian, might have been in the firing line.

The Escort was parked about a hundred yards up the lane, beside a gate whose top bar was broken. They made me and Smith get in the back. Brian drove. Sammy Jo lit a cigarette and rested the gun on the back of her seat. It was pointing at Smith, and both the gun and the hand that held it were trembling.

Of course we had no idea where they were taking us. My money was on a city: London, if their accents were anything to go by, but it could just as easily be Birmingham or Bristol or Manchester or Cardiff. Everything was so confused. Somehow Frances had to fit into this, though how was anyone's guess. Who was the woman they were after? And who was the man who scared the wits out of Brian and Sammy Jo? We'd gone to Youlgreave Barton in search of answers, and all we'd found were more questions.

"The Dynamic Duo," Smith murmured out of the side of her mouth, "get snatched."

"What was that?" Sammy Jo said.

"A joke," I explained. "One of those things you laugh at."

A stupid bit of dialogue, I know. But it made me feel we we't completely cowed. Not quite.

Brian drove back down the lane, past Youlgreave Barton and the Mill, and turned right on to the B road – away from Quanton St John and the town beyond. In a few miles I knew the road would run into an A road going north-south. Once we hit that, I should be able to get a better idea of our destination.

But we never got there. After about a mile, we turned off the B road and on to another lane, marked "Tirtle Farm Only". We never reached the farm either. Brian swung the Escort up a little cul-de-sac that led to a ruined barn. Beside the barn was a beige caravan.

He switched off the lights and killed the engine.

"Here we are," Sammy Jo said. "And thank God for that. Home, sweet home."

Suddenly a shape moved on the nearside of the car. Sammy Jo's door was opened – so sharply that she had to grab the seatback to stop herself from falling out. The interior light came on.

The gun twitched in Sammy Jo's hand. I pulled Smith out of her corner on to my lap.

"Good evening," a man said pleasantly. "You've got company, I see."

He crouched down. Despite the light from the car, he was just a black silhouette. Even his head was black – his hair, his skin, the lot. The only features he had were two strongly-marked eyebrows above two bright blue eyes.

The eyes met mine. They made me think of diamonds, ice and knives, all mixed up into something that scared me more than Sammy Jo's gun. Something that wasn't quite human. I squeezed Smith so hard she grunted. I stared back.

"Mr V!" Sammy Jo tittered awkwardly. "You gave me quite a turn."

He ignored her. "Chris Dalham, I suppose. And you must be Drew Smith's daughter. I do hope that someone's got a very good explanation."

The hissing voices went on and on. It was like being next door to a trio of snakes.

The caravan could be partitioned into two rooms.

They'd shunted us into the bedroom half while they had their summit meeting. Smith and I sat side by side on the unmade bed. The decor was totally impersonal, apart from an empty bottle of Haig and an ashtray crowded with lipstick-ringed stubs.

In better light, "Mr V" had been slightly less impressive. He was wearing black from head to foot – from Balaclava helmet to Dr Martens. Apart from the eyes, he had everything covered, even his hands. I tried to persuade myself he looked really stupid, like a grown-up playing Batman.

It was impossible to hear what they were saying. It was all in whispers. You could just about distinguish the tones: Brian blustering, Sammy Jo whining and Mr V laying down the law. Occasionally a glass clinked and twice there was the scrape of a match. Sammy Jo sometimes came across loud and clear: "It's not *our* fault . . ." You didn't have to be a genius to figure out that there was a battle of wills going on, and that the stranger was winning.

"Did you notice the bleach?" Smith whispered in my ear.

"The what?"

"That guy's eyebrows join above the nose. But he's bleached the hair so it isn't obvious. Can you beat it?"

Okay, so the bloke added vanity to the list of his antisocial characteristics. Trust a girl to come up with something so unimportant.

I opened my mouth to say so. But I never got a chance. There was a *bang-bang-bang* on the side of the caravan.

"Good evening! Anyone at home?"

The voice was so loud they must have been able to hear it in the next county. It was oozing with a sort of come-all-ye-faithful enthusiasm. I didn't know whether I should be thankful or just scared even further out of my wits.

"Oh God," I said. "Here's the Rabid Rector."

Mr V burst into the little bedroom.

"Not a whimper out of either of you," he said hoarsely, "or by God you'll regret it."

In a second he was behind us. Smith cleared her throat. I looked at her. A gun was resting on her shoulder, the barrel like a black slug nuzzling her neck. I felt sick.

We heard Brian opening the door of the caravan.

"Good evening," boomed the Rector. "My name's Gisburn. Not too late for a call, I hope? Just thought I'd pop in."

"Very kind, I'm sure," Brian said uncertainly. "Look, I'm afraid the wife's not feeling too good – "

"I'm sorry to hear that." Gisburn's voice was even louder. He had actually muscled his way into the caravan. "What's the problem?"

"A headache," Sammy Jo said.

"That's it, a headache," Brian said. "So you see – "

"I wouldn't be surprised if the sunshine is something to do with it. Bit of fresh air, that's my advice. Lovely night for a stroll, eh? I'd avoid tobacco and alcohol, too. Perhaps a couple of aspirin just before bed. Quite a heatwave we're having. Have you come far?"

"London." Brian sounded sulky.

"I like to welcome our visitors, you know. I hope we'll see you in church on Sunday. I've brought a copy of the parish magazine. Only 20p. All proceeds to the Church Restoration Fund."

"I don't think – "

"Buy one, Brian," Sammy Jo ordered. "All in a good cause."

Coins rattled in the next room.

"Keep the change," Brian said.

"Very civil of you," Gisburn said. "These caravans are miracles of ingenuity, aren't they? So much crammed into so little space. Is that the bedroom through there?"

Mr V slithered off the bed and crouched beside the door. Gisburn was quite capable of barging in if he felt like it. The Rabid Rector had his faults but lack of personality wasn't among them. Brian and Sammy Jo were outclassed.

At least Sammy Jo tried to stop him. "It's in a terrible state."

Smith's hand went round in an arc. It grabbed the neck of the empty whisky bottle, swept upwards and suddenly changed direction. Simultaneously she flung herself off the bed.

The bottle hit Mr V just above the right ear.

It was all astonishingly quiet. The Balaclava softened the thud of the blow. The bottle didn't break. Mr V grunted and toppled sideways against the corner of the bed. He moaned and began to sit up.

Smith opened the door a crack – Mr V's leg was wedged against it – and slipped out of the bedroom. I followed. Mr V tried to hook his arm round my leg. Suddenly he gave up. He must have realized it was too late. He couldn't get us back without revealing himself to Gisburn.

Brian and Sammy Jo gaped at us.

"Good evening to you!" Gisburn had apparently forgotten the circumstances of our last meeting. "You're staying at the Mill, aren't you?"

"That's right," Smith said. "Just passing through." She turned to Sammy Jo. "Thanks for having us – we'd better be getting back now. Bye."

She opened the outside door and jumped down. A second later we were running down the lane. The night air was sweet and soft. At the junction where the lane met the road to Tirtle Farm, an elderly Morris Traveller was parked on the verge. I guessed it was Gisburn's.

"Let's wait for him," I said. "They won't dare do anything, not while he's around."

"No, come on."

"But Smith – "

She didn't wait to argue the toss. She ran on. I assumed she was heading for the B road. But halfway down the hill she stopped and began to climb over a gate on the lefthand side.

By this time I was feeling pretty annoyed with her. I went after her, of course. On the other side she jogged off through what felt like a field of corn. I stumbled along in her wake. There were a few stars overhead but no moon. It was hard going and after a few yards she stopped and crouched down.

I joined her. "Do you think you could spare a minute to tell me what you're up to?" I said coldly.

"Sshh!" she said.

Someone was starting a car engine.

"That's the Morris," I said.

We listened to it spluttering down the hill. Then the sound of the Morris was overlaid by the much nearer engine of the Escort.

"I thought so," Smith said. "They're not wasting any time coming after us. But they'd need dogs to find us here."

She sounded so smug I could have throttled her. Sometimes she acts as if the only person capable of making decisions is herself; she doesn't even bother to consult me. It does wonders for the ego. Her ego.

So I let rip: "Okay, it was a good idea to get off the road. You handled that bottle like you'd been practising for years. And I just *loved* the way you thanked Sammy Jo for having us. But why the hell are we in the middle of a field when we could be heading for the nearest police station in Gisburn's car?"

"Because Gisburn's probably working with Frances."

"For God's sake," I said impatiently. "He's an old clergyman. How could he be mixed up in anything?"

"Listen – it figures. Frances is up to something, right? She's the one who brought us down here. She and Gisburn are Keystone Trusties, so they've got that in common from the start. Gisburn chucks us out of Youlgreave Barton, and Frances does her best to make sure we do what he says. Brian and Sammy Jo were looking for a woman in there. Okay, suppose Gisburn and Frances were keeping a prisoner in there, and Mr V wants to get hold of her."

"But – "

"Then Frances tells Gisburn about Brian and Sammy Jo. And he turns up at the caravan to check them out for himself. He leaves the car down the lane so they don't have advance warning. Come on, Chris, you got to admit it makes sense. Do you think Gisburn calls on every tourist in the area? Forcing his way in?"

"I wouldn't put it past him," I said.

"He didn't come see us at the Mill, did he?"

She made it all sound so plausible. Still, I wasn't convinced. Gisburn was a holy terror; but everything about him – his job, his accent, his age, even his church-warden – made it clear that he was a Pillar of the Establishment. It was like saying the Archbishop of Canterbury was running an extortion racket on the side: not impossible, but it just didn't seem likely.

I said all that but I couldn't shift her.

"What's the time?" she said suddenly.

"Just after eleven. Why?"

"Dad could be back. If he's not there when we get to the Mill, we'll go on to Quanton St John and raise the cops."

"And how do we get there? If Mr V's got any sense, he's patrolling the roads for us. Gisburn, too, if you're right."

"No need to go by road. Much safer overland. Anyway, it's a much shorter walk."

I glanced at the blackness around us. A few piddling little stars weren't much use. No roads, no lights, no street-signs. No one to ask. It was like a dark desert. We could walk for miles and end up nowhere.

"Just one little detail," I said. "How do we know where to go?"

"We go that way." Smith pointed into the night. "I was looking at Frances' OS map. It's just up a hill and down the other side. We can navigate by the stars." She added without much sign of modesty: "I got orienteering skills."

"How long do you reckon it'll take?" I said.

"To reach the Mill? Thirty minutes. Less if we're lucky."

We weren't lucky. And maybe Smith's orienteering skills weren't quite as finely-honed as she thought. The journey took us nearly two hours.

It was as packed with incident as an SAS assault course. There was the barbed wire fence where I left half my shirt. The stream where Smith slipped and fell in the mud. The place where we met a group of dark, snuffling shapes that seemed approximately the same size as London taxis and vaguely hostile to intruders. The nettles that stung every square inch of bare flesh they could find. The trees whose branches slapped us round the face. The fields we crossed that seemed to have no gates in the thick, thorny hedges that enclosed them.

We had to make a lot of detours. Every now and then Smith glanced up at the sky. Twice she decided we'd been following the wrong star. They all looked the same to me.

Another thing was the need to move as quietly as possible. You just wouldn't believe that two people on a starlit country ramble could make so much noise. At first I thought every shadow was Mr V, waiting patiently for us. Soon I stopped caring.

It was a relief when we started going downhill. "Not far now," Smith said. 40 minutes later we bumped into a hedge. "Maybe one more field," Smith said. "We should hit the lane between the Mill and Youlgreave Barton."

We worked our way along the hedge and found a gate. Beyond the gate was a lane, not a field. It wasn't just any old gate: the top bar was broken. This was the place where Brian and Sammy Jo had left the Escort when they broke into Youlgreave Barton. The Mill was still a quarter of a mile away.

"Minor navigational deviation," Smith said. "Or maybe the map was out of date."

"More like a simple case of pilot error," I said. "At least we can walk back along the lane."

"Don't be stupid," she said. "We'll keep to the fields as long as we can."

That took another 20 minutes. But I have to admit she was right. As we were passing Youlgreave Barton, the Escort suddenly came to life on the other side of the hedge. I heard two doors close. The car drove off towards the Mill. Its headlamps sent prickles of light through the hedge.

The Escort stopped by or near the Mill. Another door banged. The car moved off again towards the B road.

Three doors. Three people: Mr V, Brian and Sammy Jo. In theory we were safe.

I whispered to Smith, who was a few yards ahead of me: "They've checked Youlgreave Barton and the Mill. For us – or the woman?"

"Both, I guess."

"But if you're right, and if they found Frances and Drew at the Mill – "

She stopped so suddenly that I bumped into her. Her face was a pale smudge against the hedge.

"Do you think – ?"

"I don't know what to think," I hissed back.

Smith broke into a run. She'd glimpsed the same

possibility as I had. Mr V must be getting desperate. He wouldn't have treated Frances or Drew with kid gloves if he'd found them at the Mill. Especially if Smith was right and Frances was a sort of rival. Especially if he thought Frances knew where the woman was.

When we got there, the Mill was in darkness. We retreated a few yards up the hill. We paused at a tiny triangle of wasteland, a dip in the middle of the field, and sheltered behind the solitary tree that grew there. We had a good view of the house and yard – as good as you could have in this light. The Peugeot wasn't there.

"They can't have come back yet," Smith said. You wouldn't have thought a whisper could sound relieved, but hers did.

"So we go on to the village and find a cop?" I said. The thought of yet another, even longer cross-country journey did nothing for my morale. "Do you want to leave a note at the Mill?"

The tree beside us cleared its throat.

"I wouldn't do that if I were you," it said.

CHAPTER NINE

"Three doors closed," Gisburn murmured. "But only two people were in the car."

Even when he whispered there was something in his voice that made you feel he was addressing an audience: captive parishioners or a regiment on parade.

"How do you know?" I managed to say.

"The man with the beer belly and all those chains is still there. Brian, is it? He's sheltering in the lee of the outside steps. Careless sort of chap: if you watch for a moment, you'll see his cigarette."

We were too stunned to do anything but follow his suggestion. Sure enough a red spot glowed briefly in the yard.

"They've got walkie-talkies," the Rector went on. "The woman and the other man have driven down to the Rectory. I heard them talking about it. It's a bit of a problem, I must admit."

To hear him talk you'd have thought he was telling the Women's Institute about a little difficulty with the greenfly on his roses.

Smith grabbed my arm. "Come on, Chris."

"Do wait a moment," Gisburn almost pleaded. "By the way, I must apologize for shouting at you yesterday. There was a reason for it."

"Oh yeah," I said. "The black woman you and Frances have been keeping at Youlgreave Barton?"

"You know about her?" The bark was back in his voice. "How? Did Frances tell you?"

"We figured it out for ourselves," Smith said. "What the hell are you two up to? Do *you* want to tell us, or shall we ask the police?"

Gisburn said "*Gorwhumphah*" in a thoughtful sort of way.

"What made you turn up at the caravan?" I said, trying to keep him on the defensive; the only thing we had in our favour was the fact he didn't want us to go to the police.

"Eh? Oh, Frances told me about them, and I thought I'd better look them over."

One old man, I thought unwillingly, dropping in on three very unpleasant people: okay, so he had guts as well as personality.

"But what on earth were *you* doing there?" he went on.

"We kind of coincided at Youlgreave Barton," Smith said. "Sammy Jo and Brian ran into us. The other guy, Mr V, turned up later, at the caravan."

"Mr V?" Gisburn sounded breathless.

"That's what they called him."

"What did he look like?"

"His face was covered all the time," I said. "A Balaclava helmet – you know, like terrorists wear."

"He was in the bedroom with you all the time I was there? How did you – ?"

"His head hit a bottle," Smith said. "Well, I guess we'll be off now."

"No – look: these people are dangerous. You see, it's all out in the open now. We know who they are, and they know who we are. They can't afford to hang around. I imagine they were going to use you as hostages – propose some sort of deal."

"Let's go tell the police about it."

"I can't let you go to the police," Gisburn said unhappily.

"But those guys have got *guns*," Smith said. "You know? Bang-bang, you're dead?"

The Rector grunted, as if the news came as no surprise to him, and went on with his own train of thought: "You can't go back to the Mill. I can't leave you at the Rectory.

There'd be too many explanations if I took you to someone's house . . . Anyway, the car's probably out of action now."

"How come?" I asked.

Gisburn waved in the direction of the lane. "They found it down there. I heard them lifting the bonnet. I imagine they've ripped out the HT lead or something. I know it's a lot to ask, but will you trust me? Frances would want you to."

Smith muttered something that sounded like "Stuff Frances."

"What about Drew?" I said.

"Oh, he'd agree. He's not directly involved with this but he knows what's happening. He's very sympathetic to our – um – aims, I assure you."

I said, "And why should we believe you?"

"I'm afraid you'll just have to take my word for it," Gisburn said. "I can't *prove* that Drew would agree with me. Of course, it's unlikely he and Frances would be together in the first place unless they had similar – um – ideals."

"Ideals?" Smith seized on the word. "Are you saying this is a – what do you call it? – a matter of conscience?"

"You could call it that, I suppose. Sounds a little pretentious but there you are."

Sometimes you've got to trust your intuition about people because there's no other way to come to a decision about them. Intuitions change, just like everything else. In the last few minutes the Rabid Rector had turned into something more like an Old English sheepdog. He had a nasty bark but I didn't think he was likely to bite.

"Okay," I said. "I'll believe you."

Smith made a neutral sound that was marginally nearer to yes than no.

"So what do we do?" I asked.

"There's only one safe place within easy reach," Gisburn said. "And that's what you might call the eye of the storm. Oscar's Castle."

"Hi," said the red-haired hippie with a pony tail. "I'm Kev the Rev."

Gisburn did one of his more restrained *Gorwhum-phahs*. "Kevin is a clergyman too," he explained. "These days – um – we come in all shapes and sizes."

It was three-quarters of an hour later and we were standing in a shack on the edge of the encampment in Oscar's Castle. The final stage of the walk had been relatively easy. Gisburn seemed to know every corner of the countryside round here, and he'd led us up to Oscar's Castle as easily as if it had been broad daylight. On the way he'd pumped everything we knew out of us.

I don't know if "shack" is the right word for the place where Kev the Rev lived. It was roughly circular and seemed to be supported by a framework of branches and old iron. Part of the wall had once been a tent. Another part consisted of cardboard boxes; THIS WAY UP one of them said, upside down. There were reeds on the floor with blankets spread on top. Two deckchairs with faded canvas stood near the wall. A brightly-coloured blanket was draped from ceiling to floor. Behind it, I imagined, was Kev the Rev's bedroom. A single candle lantern provided the light. It was surprisingly cosy.

Gisburn didn't introduce us to Kev the Rev. All he said was: "Where is she?"

Kev nodded at the blanket. "You can come out now," he called.

The blanket twitched. A stockily-built black woman slipped past it – cautiously, like a cat on unfamiliar territory, unsure of its welcome.

"Hello, my dear," Gisburn said. "Everything all right?"

She looked blankly at him and didn't answer. Her expression was answer enough: it said *How can anything be all right?* She had short hair and she was wearing jeans

80

and a jumper. I don't know what I'd been expecting. What I hadn't expected was someone who looked so completely ordinary.

"Some ghost," I muttered to Smith, who was standing just in front of me.

"This is Jenny," Gisburn said. "Not her real name, in fact."

"Jenny," Smith said. "As in Jenny Black?"

Gisburn blinked at her, then nodded. "Kevin, before we go on with this, I've got an errand for you. Would you cycle down to the village and phone the Poignton Manor Hotel? Frances and Drew are having dinner there. Tell them to come and meet us here. It's vital that they don't go back to the Mill."

"What?"

Kev was miles away. Gisburn repeated what he had said. Kev beamed and said, "Sure thing!" He practically ran out of the shack. It was as if he was hugging something to himself, something we couldn't see. For a second, Gisburn stared after him; I think he'd got the same impression and it puzzled him too.

Then he looked at Jenny. "Bad news, I'm afraid. Viljoen's arrived. He kidnapped Smith and Chris – I presume he planned to propose a straight swap."

Jenny's lips tightened. She sat down in one of the deckchairs. More like fell into it.

Smith said: "Can you *please* tell us what all this is about?"

Gisburn nodded and said to Jenny, "We might as well. I'm sure they won't talk."

Jenny just shrugged. And at that moment she stopped being ordinary. I suddenly realized that she hadn't said anything because she couldn't trust herself to speak: she was too scared.

"Have you heard of the Underground Railroad?" Gisburn said to me and Smith.

I shook my head.

But Smith said: "Like in American history? The organization that helped runaway slaves escape from the South?"

"Precisely."

"But there aren't any runaway slaves," I said. "Not these days."

"Aren't there? Nowadays we have political refugees instead. And people who are being kept apart from their families because they don't have the right passport. Not so very different."

Smith was frowning. "You're saying there's an Underground Railroad here?"

"Not just in Britain. In other European countries too. And there's a thriving sanctuary movement in the States."

"But what is it?" I said.

"Just a loose network of individuals, communities, churches. People who believe they have a duty to give shelter to refugees." He paused. "Even when it means breaking the laws of their own country. Sometimes we've looked after people for years. Often we hide them in rural areas like this – the authorities are less likely to pick them up."

Suddenly a lot of things made sense. If you were trying to hide a black woman in the English countryside, where better than a house that was reputedly haunted by one? Also, if Jenny were some sort of illegal immigrant, Gisburn and Frances couldn't afford to go to the police about Viljoen and Co, because that would mean betraying her.

"If Jenny goes back to her own country, she will be tortured, probably killed," Gisburn said. "Not because of what she's done. It's who she is, whom she's related to. She came here on a tourist visa a few months ago. Frances helped her apply for asylum, but the authorities turned the application down. So we had no alternative."

Beside me Smith was staring at the ground. I don't know about her but I was feeling awful. A few hours ago

Gisburn and Frances were very nearly at the top of my hate-list.

"If she's a refugee," Smith said, "why was the application turned down?"

Gisburn shrugged. "Officially because she's not entitled to citizenship, and because they didn't consider her life was in danger if she went back to her own country. Unofficially there were other reasons. There's the general point that the Home Office isn't exactly enthusiastic about black immigrants. And in Jenny's case, giving her asylum might complicate some very delicate negotiations between this country and hers. Apparently we're trying to sell them some tanks and surface-to-air missiles. There's a lot of money involved."

"Okay," Smith went on. "But how does Viljoen come into this? And Brian and Sammy Jo?"

"Viljoen has been hired to kill Jenny. I believe he's a professional killer."

"Hired by her own government?"

"At a few removes, I imagine."

"Why bother?" I said. "Why not let the British send her back to them?"

"Because they can't be sure the British will find her. Because Jenny's father was a leading opposition politician. Because they are terrified that Jenny will act as a focus for opposition to the regime."

All this time, Jenny was just sitting there – not even watching us. Fear does terrible things to people. It sort of makes them less human. There was a kid at our school once – a couple of years younger than me. He got bullied a lot. They called him "The Brown Slug". After a couple of months he wasn't really human any more. He even looked like a slug.

"Viljoen," Gisburn went on, "hired Brian and Sammy Jo to help him trace Jenny. Probably they guessed Frances might still be in touch with her, which is why they followed you down to Quanton St John. We gathered what they were up to, and arranged with Kevin to move Jenny here. If we'd left her another hour at Youlgreave Barton, it would have been too late."

It wasn't a pleasant thought. One terrified woman alone in that derelict house. Brian and Sammy Jo breaking in. And behind them was Viljoen, a.k.a Mr V, doing his impersonation of Batman on the side of evil.

"I'm asking you to break the law," Gisburn said. "Even by keeping quiet about this you'll be accessories. Will you do it?"

Smith said: "Why are *you* doing it?"

For a few seconds Gisburn said nothing. He looked uncomfortable, as some people do when they have to talk about their beliefs. Then: "You know, in the 1930s, a lot of Jews wanted to come to England from Germany. Our official policy was to keep them out. After the war, when everyone did their arithmetic, it came out that six million Jews died in the camps. Some of those could have been alive today, living in England. We turned our backs on them. We have no excuse for making the same mistake again."

Suddenly Jenny spoke: "Render unto Caesar."

It was a shock to hear her voice. The words sounded as though they'd been wrenched out of her against her will.

Gisburn almost squirmed with embarrassment. It was funny that a clergyman of all people should mind talking about morality. Imagine a doctor getting embarrassed by illnesses, or a teacher by a class full of kids.

"'Render unto Caesar what is Caesar's,'" he said at last; "'unto God what is God's.' But the point is that sometimes both God and Caesar make conflicting demands. The state says one thing and your conscience says another. The dilemma's as old as the hills. You don't have to believe in God, of course, just that some things are right and others are wrong."

"What you're saying," Smith said, "is that if both God

and Caesar lay claim to the same thing, you got to give God the right of way?"

"It's your choice," Gisburn said, which wasn't much help. "It always is."

Smith started to say something but Gisburn held up his hand. A pushbike was rattling towards the shack. Trust Kev the Rev to have an ecologically sound means of transport. A second later he burst in.

"Well," Gisburn said, "Did you get through?"

"No, as a matter of fact – they'd just left. But I phoned Jim Hingham instead."

"You did *what*?" said Gisburn, and suddenly the Old English sheepdog had turned back into a rabid Rottweiler.

Kev the Rev took a step backwards and bumped into one of the branches by the doorway; the whole shack shuddered.

"Look, I know we haven't discussed it, but I suddenly thought: that's it! The Press! I mean, if we can get the nationals interested – and it's a good human-interest story, so I don't see why we shouldn't – Jenny will be as safe as houses. Jim's only on the local rag but he acts as a stringer for at least two nationals. So I thought: why not give him a buzz? No harm done. And in fact it might even do *us* a bit of good: the Planning Department is trying to evict us again, and we could do with some good publicity. And I was right. Jim was fascinated: he's going to come up right away."

I was watching Gisburn: his face was turning darker and darker. I thought he was going to explode – literally. But when he spoke it was so softly that I could hardly make out the words.

"Do you realize that Hingham is practically an honorary policeman? He gets his bread and butter from them. He's even a Special Constable. Do you really think he's going to keep quiet about this?"

He turned away and lifted the sheet of polythene that

blocked the doorway. The next shack was about twenty yards away. The noises of the camp drifted towards us. Someone was playing a guitar. A child laughed. People were talking: just a rumble of voices, no words. A dog barked. In the distance there were a few cars on the road between the town and Quanton St John.

But one of the engines – no, two of them – were nearer. I could see their lights. Two cars were picking their way along the track that led from the road to Oscar's Castle.

Kev the Rev cleared his throat. "Is that Jim?"

"Perhaps," Gisburn said. "And it looks like he's brought his friends with him."

CHAPTER TEN

The crisis had a weird effect on Gisburn. Suddenly he looked about ten years younger and two feet taller.

"Kevin," he snapped. "Does Hingham know about me?" He nodded at Smith and me. "Or these two?"

Kev the Rev shook his head. The ponytail wagged from side to side.

"Let's keep it that way. What about Youlgreave Barton and Frances?"

"No – there wasn't time to say much – "

"Well, that's something. When they arrive, just say that when you got back Jenny had gone. All right?"

The cars were getting nearer. Their headlights snaked round the zigzags of the track. Their engines were grinding along in first gear – the surface was better suited to tractors, and the slope was much steeper on this side of the hill than it was on the side facing Youlgreave Barton. But on they came, closer and closer. All the dogs of Oscar's Castle had woken up to bark at them.

Jenny ducked behind the curtain while Gisburn was talking. She came back with a British Airways flight bag and an army-surplus jacket. Then she waited to be told where to run to. It struck me that this was what her life had been like for the last few months, maybe longer: between them, the authorities and the Underground Railroad made all the decisions for her. She was already in a kind of prison.

"In theory you could stay here," Gisburn said to me and Smith. "But I think it'd be better for all concerned if you came with me."

Better for Jenny, I think he meant. He couldn't trust us, not really – he didn't know us well enough.

"What are we waiting for?" Smith said.

Gisburn led the way, moving at a fast walk. Then Jenny, then Smith, then me limping along behind them. First we followed the route we had come by – diagonally across a long, gently sloping field to the gate at the bottom. Here Gisburn paused. There was a rustle of paper. Then, instead of carrying on to Youlgreave Barton, he swung left and took us over a stile.

We were in a sort of tunnel between two hedges, so overgrown that in places they met in the middle above our heads. Once upon a time maybe it had been a footpath. It was so dark that we went along it in a human chain. Gisburn slowed the pace – the tunnel was choked with weeds and fallen branches. Something got up my nose and I sneezed. Nobody said anything but their silence was like a reproof.

I guessed we were following the contours of the hill; the path was bumpy but it wasn't going noticeably up or down. I couldn't see much besides the grey blur of Smith in front of me; and all I heard were leaves rustling, the snap of branches, my own breathing and, once, far above us in Oscar's Castle, the sound of a man shouting wordlessly.

Gisburn stopped abruptly. We clustered round him. It was no longer so dark: we'd reached the end of the tunnel. A barbed-wire fence stretched across the mouth. Beyond it was another of those endless fields. And beyond that was a dark and jagged mass along the skyline.

"Where are we going?" Smith said.

"Branston Spinney's over there," he whispered back. "A stream runs through it, the one that comes down at the Mill. It's quite shallow and it's got a sandy bottom. I want us to wade downstream and – "

"Why are we going paddling?" Smith said. She's the kind of person who doesn't take easily to military discipline; she wants to have reasons for everything.

"To confuse the dogs, of course," Gisburn said in a

matter-of-fact way that made me feel unwell. "I've already used pepper to cover our scent, and I'll scatter some more as we go – that'll help. Anyway, the stream divides in the middle of the wood, and makes a little island before it joins up again. There's a dead oak tree on the lefthand bank – you can reach it from the water. It's got a sort of platform in the middle of it, about six feet above the ground. I use it for bird-watching sometimes."

We were halfway across the field when Jenny put one hand on Gisburn's arm and the other on Smith's.

"Listen."

It was only the second thing she'd said to us.

"I can't hear anything," Gisburn said after a moment. Nor could I.

"Something's moving along the bottom of the field."

"Livestock?" Gisburn said.

"No. Men. Two of them, I think. In the same direction as us."

"It must be a hundred yards away. You can't be sure."

"You see that? The torch?"

A tongue of light flicked along a gate in the hedge. It was there for three seconds at most. Just the light: no sign of the men behind it.

Gisburn swore softly. For a clergyman he had a lot of unexpected habits.

"I bet we've got Anthorn to thank for this," he said. "Come on. Run."

We jogged across the field as quietly as we could. I had a stitch and I was quietly praying for this whole business to end. It looked like the police had sent in the cars at the front and put men on foot at the back. Our only chance of putting off Jenny's arrest (and ours) was to reach the wood before the police did. And what then? Once it was daylight, they'd find us in about five minutes. We were on a hiding to nothing. I reached the point where I hardly cared what happened to me as long as a hot bath and a bed were part of the package.

Disaster hit us just before we reached the boundary of the field. There was a crash. A howl of pain. Gisburn said a couple of words at full volume; a boy at our school was chucked out for saying the same thing to the Head.

Of course we all stopped. He was on the ground, curled over and clutching his right leg. Beside him was something that looked like a chunk of agricultural machinery. He must have slammed into it at full speed.

"Get into – " He sobbed with pain and sucked in some breath. " – the wood." Another sob. "*Hide*."

Jenny said: "They're coming."

This time we all heard them; the two men were pounding up the field, no longer trying to be quiet. Jenny yelped almost noiselessly and darted towards the wood.

"Wait," Gisburn said. "The pepper."

He passed the bag to Smith. Then we sprinted after Jenny.

If there'd been a hedge or barbed wire or even a serious fence, we would have been too late. Instead there were just horizontal strands of wire stretched between wooden stakes. We struggled through and into Branston Spinney.

I don't know what the others did. I stayed on my belly and wriggled forwards like a demented worm for about ten seconds. Then I stopped and tried to press myself into the cool, spongy leaf mould that covered the ground. A root was digging into my left hip, so hard that it left a bruise, and at the time I hardly noticed.

The running feet were much louder. Torchlight flickered through the leaves.

"Okay," a man said, his voice hoarse with a kind of gloating triumph. "Let's have a look at you."

"Who's that?" Gisburn said. His voice was almost back to normal though he was obviously still in pain.

"Police. Hey, aren't you – ?"

"Splendid!" Gisburn said. "Good of you to come along, officer. Most opportune."

"What do you mean?" The man added "Sir" as an afterthought.

"Didn't you hear me shouting? I walked straight into this damned seed drill. *Gorwhumphah*. It's my leg. I don't think I can walk."

The cop made a quick recovery. "You wouldn't like to tell me what you're doing out here at this time of night?"

"Eh? Looking for badgers, of course. There used to be a sett in Branston Spinney. You interested in badgers? I did one of my 'Nature Notes' about them in the Parish Magazine last year. I'll let you have a copy. And what are you doing out here? Not poachers again?"

"No, sir, not exactly. Er – I can't go into details."

"Why on earth not?" Gisburn said. "Don't I know you? Shine that torch on your face." There was a pause. "I thought so. Dean Riddle, isn't it? I've a bone to pick with you, young man. Saw your mother last week in that damned nursing home they stuffed her into, and she's very lonely. Why haven't you been to see her?"

Riddle muttered something about work.

"Nonsense. Even sergeants don't work twenty-four hours a day. *Gorwhumphah*. Well, what are you waiting for?"

"Sorry, sir?"

"Help me up. You and your colleague should be able to manage an old man. I think I can just about hobble along with my arms round your shoulders. I presume you weren't proposing to leave me here all night?"

Riddle tried to get out of it by promising to summon help over his radio, but Gisburn wasn't having that. He grabbed the radio himself and talked to whoever was in charge at Oscar's Castle. Gisburn assured him that he'd seen and heard no one but Riddle and his sidekick in the last half hour. He also said he'd catch a chill if he was forced to lie on the damp grass until a stretcher came.

A moment later Gisburn and the two policemen moved

slowly away with Gisburn talking loudly to them so that
we knew exactly where they were. Slowly his voice was
submerged by the rustles of the night. The sweat on my
skin cooled and I began to shiver.

"Chris?"

I raised my head and stared in the direction of the
whisper. "Smith?"

"Over here. Jenny?"

"Here." Her voice seemed to be about three inches
away from my elbow. "The stream's on my left."

Jenny's night vision seemed to be as good as her
hearing. She slipped through the trees to the bank of the
stream. For all the noise she made, she might have been
a genuine ghost. Smith and I fumbled after her.

The water made very little sound – it was just another
rustle among the crowd. Smith suggested we took off our
shoes and socks.

It was freezing. The water came up to my knees. I'd
rolled up my jeans as far as they would go but the
bottoms got soaked. We edged down the stream. It was
so dark that we might as well have been blind. At each
step I expected to put my foot on something unpleasant
and/or painful, and usually I wasn't disappointed. After
I'd stubbed a few toes it got slightly better: my feet
were so cold I hardly cared what else was happening to
them.

Jenny was still in the lead, which was just as well. Left
to myself I'd have walked right past the island, let alone
the oak tree.

The pressure eased off when we got to the tree.
Climbing it was like climbing a ladder, even in the
darkness. Gisburn or someone had cut toeholds in the
bark. Most of the top of the tree had fallen off. All that
was left was this roughly circular platform, hollowed out
of the main trunk.

Once inside we crouched down in a tangle of legs and
bodies. The first thing Jenny did was unzip her bag and

produce a bar of chocolate. I don't think any food I've had has ever tasted so good. We munched away and tried to pretend we were getting warmer.

"Mr Gisburn will send help in the morning," Jenny said. "I wish he'd found us somewhere more comfortable. Can you move your leg a bit?"

"Maybe we won't be here in the morning," I said, squeezing closer to Smith to give Jenny a few more square inches of legroom. At that moment something about her irritated the hell out of me. I knew we had to help her. But she seemed to take the help for granted, as her right.

"We got to *do* something," Smith said. "Maybe even talk to the cops."

Jenny sort of squawked.

"No, listen," Smith went on. "We got to think this out. What's Viljoen going to do when he can't find Jenny at the Rectory? He'll come back to the Mill, that's what. He's desperate now – he can't afford to be subtle. So he'll have to find Frances and make her tell him where Jenny is. It's the only thing he can do."

"They could all be at the Mill now," I said.

"I know. That's what's worrying me."

"Does it matter?" Jenny said. "If Frances talks, she'll send Viljoen to Oscar's Castle. He'll run smack into the police."

"The point is," Smith said in a whisper with a serrated edge, "right now Frances and my father are probably in a lot more danger than you are. And there's another thing: now Gisburn's done his leg in, Frances is the only person round here who can help you."

Jenny sniffed. "Then we'd better get hold of her."

We had a nasty little silence. Smith and I were shoulder to shoulder and I felt her breathing hard and fast. I thought about that bloody stream, the stretch of unknown country between here and the Mill, the cows, the barbed wire, the nettles, the boobytraps and the probability that

Viljoen, Sammy Jo and Brian were waiting at journey's end. And I thought about Smith and what she must be feeling.

"Okay," I said. "Suppose I go down to the Mill and find out what's happening."

"That woman," Smith said, "deserves to be shot."

"No, she doesn't," I said, though I could see what Smith meant. "If people had been hunting you for months and months, you'd get a bit selfish."

Smith shot ahead and for a while we walked in silence. We both knew that talking was a luxury we maybe couldn't afford. By night, the country is one big hiding place. This area seemed to be crawling with invisible people, most of whom I didn't want to meet.

Still, I was relieved to have company. I was almost as glad as Smith that Jenny had decided to stay in the tree. We came out of Branston Spinney, following the course of the stream and hoping that we'd hit the lane sooner rather than later. The view downhill was blocked by another clump of trees. Suddenly the land rose slightly, the trees dipped down and we saw a cluster of lights below.

"Oh God," Smith said, "Dad and Frances must be there."

The lights could only belong to the Mill – there were no other inhabited houses on the lane. It was a quarter of a mile away, across a couple of fields. Smith started to run.

I knew it was hopeless. What could we hope to do against three armed people? But I went after Smith. Someone had to stop her from mounting a one-woman suicide mission.

We were halfway down the last field when we saw the headlights. There were two pairs of them – coming at speed along the lane from the direction of the B road. Smith ran on, veering to the right towards a gate on the lane. We couldn't go directly to the Mill because the stream, which was much wider and deeper down here, was in the way.

The cars stopped by the Mill. An engine backfired. A jolt ran through me as though I'd touched a live wire.

Not a car – that was a gunshot.

I put on a spurt and grabbed Smith's arm just as she reached the gate, which was standing open. She struggled to free herself.

"Now hold on," I said. "That's got to be the police."

If there were bullets flying around there was no sense in us getting in the firing line. We'd be no help to anyone then.

She stopped fighting. I let go of her and took a step backwards into something hard and metallic. A dark-coloured vehicle was parked just inside the field. I could hardly see it because it blended in with the hedge. It was something big and boxlike, perhaps a Range Rover. There was no time to worry about that now.

"We'll get a better view from up there," I said, grabbing her hand and pulling her up the field. I didn't give a damn about the view: I just wanted to get us farther out of harm's way.

We ran back about thirty yards and dropped to the ground. There was another shot from the Mill and a woman screamed. Someone – Brian, I think – was shouting.

"Look," Smith whispered.

One of the upstairs windows of the cottage was opening. I saw a black figure crouching on the sill behind. Batman was doing a runner on his mates.

Viljoen let himself feet first out of the window and slithered down the wall until he was hanging by his fingers from the sill. Then he let go.

There was so much racket from the house that I didn't even hear the splash as he hit the stream. A few seconds later he scrambled out. He was in the same field as us. He sprinted towards us, along the line of the hedge. By now Smith and I were lying flat on the grass. For a moment I thought he must have extra-sensory perception: he'd seen us and was coming to get us.

But Viljoen swerved: he was heading for the car. A second later the engine exploded into life. He swung into the lane, scraping the gatepost, and rocketed off towards the B road.

There was another outburst of shouting at the Mill. Car doors slammed. One of the other cars reversed down the lane, backed through the gateway into the field and set off after Viljoen. And all the while Smith and I lay there.

She wriggled away from me and stood up.

"Now wait a minute," I said. "We've got to – "

I might as well have saved my breath. I stumbled to my feet and followed her. She was already through the gateway and running up the lane. A police car was parked by the gate of the Mill.

"Here! You!" someone shouted.

"Where's my father?" Smith said.

I caught up with her in the yard. Light spilled out of all the windows and through the open door. The Peugeot was in its usual place. Smith was fighting to get away from a large uniformed policeman.

My mind went blank, as though it were a stage and someone had dropped an angry red curtain in front of it. I charged. My shoulder rammed itself into the cop's waist and we all went sprawling on to the cobbles.

Inspector Anthorn appeared like a grey ghost in the doorway.

"You can let her go, Riddle. That's Mr Smith's daughter and her friend."

"Well, how was I to know?" Riddle muttered. "Come at me like a pair of bloody dervishes."

"That's enough," Anthorn said softly. "Now, you two. Inside."

The living room was full of people and one of the

windows had got itself broken since I last saw it. An acrid smell stung the back of my throat. Besides Anthorn there were two plain-clothes cops, a man and a woman. Through the open door to the kitchen I glimpsed Brian and Sammy Jo sitting at the table with a hulking great policeman between them and the door. Drew was lying on the sofa with his eyes closed. Frances knelt beside him, holding his hand. The red dress was ripped down the back and her hair was all over the place.

She looked up as we came in. Her face was pale and dirty. When she saw us she bit her lip, and for a moment I thought she was going to cry.

"Thank God you're safe," she said. "Where've you been?"

"Good question," Anthorn said. He shut the kitchen door.

Smith rushed over to her father.

"He's unconscious," Frances said. "I honestly don't think there's anything to worry about. The Inspector's sent for an ambulance."

"Well?" Anthorn said to me. "Where were you?"

"I wish I knew," I said, trying to win a little time. "What's been happening here?"

"Trouble. I'll tell you about it. First I want you to answer my question."

"Well." I summoned my powers of creativity, and as usual they came galloping to the rescue. "It was like this. Smith and I were having a walk in the field at the back – "

"At this time of night?"

"Yes," I said. I decided against adding a man-to-man leer; Anthorn wasn't the type to appreciate it. "We heard this car on the lane. Went down to see who it was. There were these people in the yard – those two" – I nodded at the kitchen – "and a man in black clothes. Anyway, they broke into the cottage and we thought we'd better get help or something."

Anthorn said: "What time was this?"

"Don't know. Didn't look at my watch. After eleven, I think. We've been wandering round in circles ever since, getting lost. We'd still be out there if we hadn't seen the headlights coming up the lane. Was that you?"

He grunted. He was about to ask me something else when Frances suddenly stood up.

"Inspector – who are these people?" she demandéd. "What's happening?"

"You don't know, Ms Byram?"

"Of course I don't. Mr Smith and I came back from dinner and we were simply set upon by these three intruders. I – "

"I believe you're a solicitor? And that you sometimes represent clients who are trying to win residential status in the United Kingdom?"

"That's correct. But – "

Anthorn held up his hand and went on in the same oddly formal way: "Perhaps you're not aware that we are looking for one of your clients – I beg your pardon, one of your *former* clients – whose presence in this country is contrary to the 1971 Immigration Act. And that further-more the woman in question is very probably in this area."

"Good Lord," said Frances. "What a coincidence."

"We have evidence to suggest that someone has been staying at Youlgreave Barton until very recently. Just up the road. The person involved also paid a visit to Oscar's Castle this evening."

"Really? Who told you that?"

"Let's call it information received, Ms Byram. And it seems that your intruders thought that you might have an idea about this person's whereabouts. Does that seem absurd to you?"

"Absolutely ridiculous."

A diversion arrived in the shape of the ambulance, with a doctor in tow. The doctor, a squat, middle-aged woman, pushed Anthorn, Smith and Frances aside and concentrated on Drew. She'd never been to charm school but she seemed to know her job.

Yes, she said, Drew would probably wake up with nothing worse than mild concussion, but she wanted him in hospital for observation. Anthorn rather reluctantly asked Frances and Smith if they wished to go with Drew in the ambulance.

Both of them said no. That puzzled me. Frances's reason was obvious: she had to stay around because of Jenny. But Smith was another matter. I looked across the room at her. She was staring down at her dad but I don't think she was really seeing him. She had something on her mind. Something that made her want to stay.

The next five minutes were confused. The ambulance crew carted Drew away. The doctor examined Frances, who seemed to have something wrong with her wrist, and then left. Meanwhile a plain-clothes man came in and had a long, whispered conversation with Anthorn. As a result of that Brian and Sammy Jo were led away under escort. They stared at the floor as they walked out of the cottage.

Then there were just the four of us – Anthorn and Frances, Smith and me. Suddenly the room was much larger. Anthorn seemed to have lost his taste for interrogating Frances, maybe because of something his colleague had said.

"I'll need to see you all tomorrow," he said, looking at Frances. "Can you be at the station by nine? We'll have to take statements."

Frances nodded at him. Without warning he rounded on me and Smith, just as I was beginning to hope that the worst was over.

"Have you seen anyone else this evening? Anyone at all?"

It was a bad moment. The worst wasn't over, certainly not as far as Jenny was concerned. The police, I realized, must know she was still somewhere in the area – probably alone and on foot. We knew they were right. And they weren't going to stop looking until they found her.

Then I had another one of my creative inspirations. "You don't mean the black woman in the car?" I said.

"What car? Why haven't you mentioned this?"

"We were going to." I sounded, and actually felt, annoyed: the secret of successful lying is to act the part you're playing; if you fool yourself, you can fool other people. "But you didn't give us time, did you? You started talking to Frances."

"Now, look here – " Anthorn yelled. Then he took a grip on himself and went back to his usual softly-softly approach. "Okay. What did you see?"

"Just as we came into the field at the back, your cars came along the lane. But we didn't know it was you, of course. We got down to the gate – you know? on to the lane? – and it was open. And there was this big car parked just inside. Range Rover – something like that. Dark colours, so you hardly noticed it against the hedge. Then the shooting started and we pulled back. Lay down, actually."

I paused for dramatic effect. So far I was keeping very close to the truth, which is always a good idea when you want to con someone.

"Very sensible," Anthorn commented. "Go on."

"Well – er." I nearly said Viljoen, a name I wasn't supposed to know. "The man in black clothes jumped out of a window into the stream. He ran round the car and drove off. The point is, when he opened the door, the interior light came on. Just for a few seconds. But there was a woman in the front passenger seat. Definitely black."

"Was she tied up? Gagged?"

I shrugged. "Didn't have time to see. Anyway we were too far away." I glanced at Smith. "Weren't we?"

"That's right," she said. "Anyway, I hardly saw her – I was looking towards the Mill."

"But you did see her?" Anthorn asked her.

"A glimpse, yeah. Then the car door slammed and that was it."

"What did she look like? What was she wearing?"

"I think she had short hair," I said, frowning with the effort of pretending to remember. "Maybe a dark jacket, but I wouldn't swear to that. Like I said, we were too far away."

Anthorn stared at me for a moment. He had uncomfortable eyes – grey like the rest of him and somehow blank, as though behind them there wasn't a mind but a collection of microchips. I couldn't tell whether or not he believed me. The longer he stared, the less likely it seemed.

"All right," he said at last. "I wish you'd mentioned this before." He looked at his watch and smothered a yawn. "I'll see you all tomorrow. Ms Byram, I'd like a word with you outside."

For a moment I thought Frances was going to refuse but she followed him out to the yard.

"I'm freezing," Smith said. "Can't we make some coffee or something?"

We went into the kitchen. I was starving so I opened the fridge. Smith ran the cold tap to fill the kettle.

Under cover of the sound of the water, she whispered: "How did the cops get here so quickly? Who told them? How come they knew so much about Frances and Jenny?"

"Well, it's not that strange – "

A car door slammed. Smith gave me a look that meant: *We'll save this till later.* We heard Anthorn drive away. Then Frances came into the kitchen and Smith asked her if she wanted coffee.

Meanwhile I found some quite normal-looking cheese in the fridge and some bread and butter in the larder. I couldn't see what was worrying Smith. Probably one of the reverends had talked.

Then the niggles started. Gisburn wasn't the chatty

type. Kev the Rev might have cracked under pressure. The trouble was, he didn't know about the stake-out at the Mill. On the other hand, maybe the police knew independently of Frances's connection with Jenny, so they'd have automatically checked the Mill when they missed her at Oscar's Castle. But why did they come in two cars and with all that manpower? It was as if they were expecting Brian and Sammy Jo, not just one frightened woman. Anthorn hadn't asked any questions about who Viljoen was – which suggested he already knew.

My brain was churning and I couldn't concentrate. Too many ifs and buts. I needed to fill the stomach to clear the mind.

"Are you okay?" Smith said to Frances.

"They just twisted my arm," Frances said. "Literally. Drew had the worst of it. That man in the Balaclava . . ." She shivered.

"Here," Smith said, passing her a mug. "Why don't you put some sugar in it?"

We all sat round the kitchen table, drinking instant coffee. Neither of the others was hungry. While I ate, they talked.

Smith said, "I guess we owe you an apology."

Frances did a double-take. "Why?"

"We know about Jenny. I think we know just about everything."

"Oh God." Frances ran her fingers through her hair, which made it look even more of a tangle than before. Under the make-up her skin was grey. I got the impression she was too shattered to feel surprised. She said in a sort of croak: "How did you find out?"

"We'll tell you later. It's a long story."

"It's such a bloody mess," Frances said. "If only Kevin had kept his mouth shut. What I'd really like to know is how Viljoen got hold of Jenny."

They both sipped their coffee. I hacked off another chunk of cheese.

"He didn't," Smith said. "Jenny's here."

Frances knocked over her mug. The coffee spread across the table and began to drip on the floor. No one moved.

"Here? You mean she's still at Oscar's Castle?"

"No," Smith said. "Here – at the Mill."

I almost choked on a mouthful of cheese.

"You'll see her if you look out of the larder window."

"In the *stream*?" Frances said.

"No – there's a little ledge between the wall and the stream. Tap on the window three times."

Frances' chair fell over. She ran into the larder and hammered on the tiny window so hard that I thought the glass was going to break.

Smith slipped out of her seat, shut the larder door and turned the key in the lock.

A double exposure is two images, the one superimposed on the other, on the same negative. A double exposure is two revelations, one on top of the other, about the same person.

"Frances is a police informer, Jenny," Smith said again, this time with a touch of exasperation. "I'll go over it again."

The internal walls of the Mill were nearly as thick as the outside ones. But even at the far end of the living room we could hear Frances banging on the larder door.

"But why?" Jenny wailed. "She helped me, she – "

"I don't know why," Smith said. "But that's not the point. The fact is, she's betrayed you, probably right from the start."

We'd fetched Jenny from the oak tree. Now she was sitting on the sofa and trying to pull her fingers off her hands. She really looked terrible.

Smith explained her line of reasoning. It started with the fact that Anthorn was so incredibly well informed about what was happening, including the reason for Brian and Sammy Jo being on the scene. He could only have got all that information from Gisburn or Frances. But it couldn't be Gisburn because in that case Anthorn would have known about our parts in the events of the night; he wouldn't have left us till he'd found out what we'd done with Jenny after Gisburn had his accident.

The next fact was that Anthorn had publicly refused to tell Frances how he knew that Jenny was at Oscar's Castle. But later, after he'd gone, Frances showed that she knew Kev the Rev was responsible for the leak. The only explanation was that Anthorn had told her when they had their private chat right at the end. If Frances were no more than a lawyer for the Underground Railroad, he had no reason to tell her anything.

When Smith first told me this, while we were still in the kitchen with Frances trying to kick down the larder door and yelling that we'd made a mistake, I'd agreed it was suspicious. But secretly I'd thought Smith was maybe allowing her dislike of Frances to make it more suspicious than it really was. Perhaps Gisburn had told the cops something but not everything. Perhaps Anthorn had other sources of information about the Underground Railroad.

Smith rooted around in Frances's handbag, which she'd taken with her to the restaurant. I wasn't convinced even when we found the missing double-exposed photograph and the negatives in the back pocket of her Filofax. Either way she'd have wanted to nick them.

Jenny was even more sceptical than I'd been. She clung to Frances like a security blanket. "You've got no *proof*," she kept saying.

"That's where you're wrong," Smith said. "You see – "

"If you're right," Jenny interrupted, "why did the police bother to raid Oscar's Castle? They knew I was there all along."

"The way I figure it, they had two reasons: one, they had to keep Hingham quiet by pretending to take the tip-off seriously; and two, things have changed since Viljoen's come on the scene. I mean, the Brits want to deport you, but letting you get murdered is another thing altogether."

"On British soil," Jenny said bitterly. "It's not such a worry if it happens elsewhere. But it doesn't prove anything. Not about Frances."

"We went looking for proof and we found it."

Smith scooped the Filofax off the floor and turned to the E page of the addresses section. She showed it to Jenny, who read out the entry Smith was pointing to.

"'U.N.Epine. 33777 (Work), 34923 (home).' Who's Epine?"

The Keystone Trust's folder of information about the Mill was on the table beside my chair. I handed it to Jenny. The folder included a list of useful phone numbers. The police station in town was among them. 33777.

"I'm doing French," Smith said. "Do you know what *une épine* means? A thorn. Anthorn."

Jenny put her head in her hands. Smith glanced at me and I guess she was feeling even worse about this than I was. After a moment Jenny sat up and blew her nose. It sounded as if she were trying to blast Frances out of her system.

"Can you drive?" Smith said.

Jenny nodded.

"Well, that's okay. You can't stay here. But there must be somewhere in London you can go to. We can use Frances's car."

"There's nowhere," Jenny said. "I've been to three safe houses in London. Frances came to see me in every one."

That was a facer. We should have thought of it before. Frances hadn't betrayed just Jenny: she would have told the police everything she could find out about the whole Underground Railroad organization in the UK – the people, the places and the way it was run.

It was 2 a.m., and I had this feeling that we'd reached the end of the road. Everything seemed dreary and hopeless.

If Viljoen found Jenny first, he'd kill her; if the cops got to her, they'd send her home – according to Jenny, to almost certain death. Thanks to Frances, we couldn't pass the buck to the Underground Railroad. Drew might have helped – I didn't believe that he'd known Frances was an informer – but he was in hospital. There was no one else to go to.

So it was down to us – me and Smith. We had an easy way and a hard way. I thought of old Gisburn and his stuff about rendering unto Caesar. It's always much more sensible to do what Caesar wants. The fact that Viljoen was on the loose even gave us a sort of excuse. Maybe Jenny was exaggerating: her government wouldn't really kill her, would they? Anyway, what could Smith and I do against the British authorities? And Caesar, in the shape of Inspector Anthorn, had another point in his favour: the fact that Jenny wasn't the easiest person in the world to like.

Smith was looking at me with those blue eyes with greeny flecks in them. I nearly laughed when I thought how differently this week was turning out from how I'd hoped. But the more I got to know her, the more I realized that where it counted we were on the same wavelength; I knew the choice she'd make and it was the same as mine. Stuff Caesar.

"All right," I said. "I can find us somewhere to stay in London. For a night at least. But God knows what we do then. I don't."

East of Oxford the sky was a clear, cool blue with red streaks along the horizon. It had a fresh sheen to it, like the glaze on a china bowl.

We stopped at a lay-by just before we hit the M40. The light wasn't really good enough but I got the camera out and took a couple of shots: one of the sky and the other of Smith looking haggard and interesting. Jenny covered her face with her hands and said, "No photos."

Dawn's a good time of day. The world is that much emptier and somehow cleaner. On the motorway I dozed off. When I surfaced again, we were cruising down the raised section of the A40, the Marylebone Flyover, and London was all around us. For a moment it was as if we were floating above a crazy carpet of buildings, streets and trees. It was all reassuringly familiar. Not a cow in sight.

"Where now?" Jenny said.

"Carry on," I said. "I'll tell you when to turn left."

"Are you sure you shouldn't call him first?" Smith asked again. She was in the front beside Jenny.

"No point. Better just to turn up."

But not at once. We had to get rid of the car. Once Frances got out of the larder, the police were going to be taking an interest in black Peugeot 205s. It was worth creating as much of a diversion as possible. I took us up beyond Camden and we dumped the car just off Kentish Town Road, on a sidestreet near a council estate. With a bit of luck someone would nick it.

We walked back to Camden Road station and caught the first westbound train of the day on the North London line. It was nearly empty – just a few people coming off nightshifts or going to work; most of them were heavily involved with their newspapers and none of them gave us a second glance. We reached Acton before seven o'clock.

The house was about ten minutes' walk from the station. The place is practically under seige by the environmental health department on account of the back garden. Well, it's not a garden anymore: just a pile of rubbish that grows and grows. The neighbours keep complaining that it's a paradise for rats, and they're probably right.

The gold 3-litre Capri was parked outside. As usual the back seat was full of cuddly animals. My sister once said that she liked a toy panda and Clive got carried away.

I leant on the doorbell. Nothing happened. I tried again. A window shot up above my head. Clive leant out, yawning. He's always yawning and it always makes me yawn too. I yawned back at him.

His head disappeared. A moment later a key flew out of the open window and clattered on the concrete path. That's what I like about Clive: no fuss, no questions and no expectations about how other people should behave. Except where Judith's concerned, he's really quite sensible.

The house is divided into two flats and he's got the one

109

at the top. He'd opened the door on the landing for us so we walked straight in. There was no sign of him. The living room was a bit more sordid than usual. Judging by the quantity of empty bottles and full ashtrays he'd been doing a lot of entertaining lately.

I went into the bedroom. Clive was huddled under the duvet on the double bed. I shook his shoulder and he looked blearily at me.

"You're early, aren't you?" he said. "The tickets are in the kitchen somewhere."

"We brought a friend," I said. "Is that okay?"

"No problem." He yawned. "Mike and Sue have gone to Glasgow. There's a spare bedroom. Unless someone else is using it."

Mike and Sue are Clive's lodgers. Mike's one of the affluent unemployed and Sue works as a sort of hostess in a sort of club off Shaftesbury Avenue.

"I thought they were in the States or Barbados or somewhere."

"They were," Clive said. "But they came back for Mike's brother's wedding. Sue took another week off work. They take weddings seriously up in Scotland."

"They won't mind us using their room?"

"They won't know. See you in the morning."

He turned over and covered his head with the duvet. I wondered when Clive's morning began. About 3 p.m.? Back in the living room Smith and Jenny were standing in stunned silence, looking at the chaos.

"That's fine," I said. "Clive's gone back to sleep."

I opened the door into the other bedroom. It was about six feet square and, compared to the rest of the place, both clean and tidy. Unfortunately there was a dead-white face and a mass of orange hair on the pillow. I muttered "Sorry" and began to back out. Suddenly I realized that the sheet covering the rest of the bed was flat: the head wasn't attached to a body.

The orange hair was a wig. The face belonged to one of

those polystyrene heads you see in shop windows. I glanced over my shoulder. Jenny was looking out of the window and Smith was investigating the kitchen. Neither of them had heard me apologizing to a hunk of polystyrene.

I followed Smith. She was putting a kettle on the stove. "This place stinks," she said. "Where does the garbage go?"

She waved a hand at thé worktop. The remains of an extensive Chinese takeaway were distributed among the usual empty milk cartons, decaying baked beans and stale crusts.

"Clive usually chucks it out of the window," I said. The kitchen was conveniently situated at the back of the house. "Just leave it. It's always like this."

Smith looked shocked. I don't think she realized that people could live in the way that Clive did. At least, I thought, no one could say we weren't educational for one another: she'd taught me about artichokes and I'd taught her about squalor.

"How much rent does he pay for this place?" she asked.

"I don't think he pays anything. It's kind of complicated."

While Smith washed three mugs in cold water – the water heater wasn't working – I searched for instant coffee, powdered milk and sugar. I came across the two Paul Anders tickets. They were pinned to the dartboard on the back of the kitchen door. What a waste of money and effort. I stuffed them in my pocket in case Clive got curious about my lack of interest in them. Not that Clive ever is curious, but there's always a first time.

Jenny was sitting in an armchair and holding out her hands to the gas fire. As we came in she looked up. At the sight of her face I felt guilty for all the negative thoughts I'd had about her.

"I might as well give myself up," she said in a tight,

111

hard voice. "I've no money and no contacts. I'll just bring trouble to you."

Smith sat cross-legged on the floor. "Is there anywhere else you'd be safe? Anywhere in the world?"

"Nowhere's safe from Viljoen."

I felt like pointing out that nowhere's safe, full stop. At any moment a car can knock you down or a brick can fall on your head. Aloud I said: "How about outside England?"

"I've got cousins in the States. But how do I get there without money and a passport?"

"You'd need a visa too," Smith said. "Our immigration laws are even tougher than the British ones. Is there someplace else you could go?"

"I've a friend in Geneva – he's a lawyer, another political exile. He'd help. He's got contacts with the Underground Railroad too."

"Can you call him?" Smith said.

"His phone's almost certainly tapped," Jenny said as if it were the most ordinary thing in the world. "I don't want to make trouble for him, too. It would be safer if I just turned up."

"Do you need a visa for Switzerland?" I said.

Jenny shrugged. "I need a visa for just about everywhere."

"You wouldn't if we could find you a British passport," Smith said.

"If – if – if. My whole life's just one big if. *If* I had a passport. *If* I had the money."

"Money's no problem," Smith said. "Not for an airfare anyway. I got my deposit account book and my cheque book."

Here I was, scraping to get together £15 for a couple of Paul Anders tickets I couldn't even use. And there was Smith with her cheque book, less concerned about buying an air ticket to Geneva than I would have been about buying a can of Coke. Maybe the money was Drew's way

112

of trying to make up for his shortcomings as a single parent.

Smith reeled off a bunch of facts and possibilities as though she were some kind of travel agent. We could get Jenny a ticket to Geneva – a return because that would make the Swiss immigration authorities less inquisitive about her – and some Swiss francs. And if we couldn't get hold of a passport today, we could give Jenny Frances's driving licence. She could use that to get into France, because France was part of the Common Market, and we could change the ticket for one to Lyon, which wasn't far from Geneva. Maybe Jenny would be able to smuggle herself across the Franco-Swiss border. If she couldn't do that, she'd have to take the risk of phoning her friend from Lyon.

It sounded impressive to me. You'd have thought Smith had spent half her lifetime making travel arrangements for refugees.

"Maybe Clive could help with a passport," I said. "He – er – knows all sorts of people."

Neither Smith nor Jenny looked too enthusiastic. I don't know what it is about Clive. He and his flat don't inspire much confidence in people.

I decided to change the subject: "What about breakfast?"

There was nothing edible in the flat so we went out to eat. Afterwards we took a bus into the West End because Smith wanted to cash a cheque and I thought it would be safer to do that in the centre of town.

We trailed back to Acton. There wasn't much point in buying an air ticket until we knew where Jenny was going to. To my surprise Clive was up when we got to the flat at about 11 o'clock. He was wandering round the living room with a towel round his waist and a dazed expression on his face.

"The phone woke me," he explained. "And then I thought I'd ring Judith at work. She said I was crazy."

I knew that already. But I could tell that Clive wanted to talk so I said, "Why?"

"Because I've got you staying with me. You'd have thought she'd be pleased."

"You didn't mention Jenny to her?"

"Eh? No, I don't think I did. Is this Jenny? How are you doing?" He focused properly on her for the first time. Only for an instant. Clive likes women to have what he calls "glamour", which wasn't Jenny's strong suit. "But Judith knew about Smith," he went on. "Your mother told her."

I had the drowning sensation I sometimes get when Clive gives me an insight into his thought processes.

"How did my mother know Smith was here?"

"Because of Smith's mum ringing up."

Smith said, "What did you say?"

She put out her hand and touched my arm. I think she was making sure that this was real, that she wasn't dreaming. She was looking at Clive, not me, her face half hopeful and half anxious. I knew why. Her mother lives in New York. Smith hasn't seen her for years.

"Her mother," I said slowly, "rang my mother up?"

"Right. To ask if Smith was there. And your mum said no, but I might know, because I told her about getting you tickets for the concert the last time I tried to phone Judith. Not this morning, I mean. Yesterday. I said you and Smith might be staying the night."

It was still as clear as mud. Obviously Clive had been trying to butter up my mother by showing he was being nice to me. All part of the campaign to win Judith back. I wondered in passing what my mother thought about me and Smith spending the night at Clive's; I was going to hear more about that.

"And then," Clive said, trying to be helpful, "Smith's mother phoned me. That's what woke me up."

114

"You mean *here*," Smith said in a strangled voice.

"Yeah – Chris's mum gave her the number. No problem – there's nothing to worry about. She just wanted to check you'd got here okay. And I said, did she want to leave a message, and she said no. Then she sort of squawked and put the phone down."

Smith sagged into the nearest chair. All the fight had been squeezed out of her. I suppose we all have our sensitive places, and Clive had just hammered a nail into hers.

"What's going on?" Jenny demanded, looking at each of us in turn.

No one answered.

I don't think Clive even heard her. Judging by his vacant expression he'd forgotten that Jenny and Smith were in the same room. Suddenly he said to me: "Well, so what did Judith say?"

"Eh?" I stared stupidly at him. Clive has this habit of assuming that his thoughts are your thoughts. "About what?"

"You said you'd tell her about the nightclub opening. You know, that place on the Fulham Road? I've got two complimentaries. You were going to sort of use your influence."

"I was going to do it this morning," I lied. "You only mentioned it yesterday afternoon. But hang on – you phoned her today. Didn't you say anything?"

"I would have done but she put the phone down on me."

"Will someone tell me what's going on?" Jenny said.

"We've got to get out of here," I said. "Now."

"Has something happened?" Clive hitched the towel more tightly around his waist. "I thought you were staying the night."

I glanced at him: he has the muscular development of an uncooked sausage and he's roughly as well-organized as a Red Setter. Hardly the Mr Macho we needed. But we didn't have any choice.

116

It wasn't difficult to figure out what had happened. Frances had escaped. She must have found our phone number in my diary upstairs at the Mill. The diary also had Clive's phone number and his address. Somehow she'd reached a phone – probably a callbox in Quanton St John – and done her anxious mother act. Now she knew where we were. What was the betting that her next call had been to Anthorn?

"When did she ring you?" I said to Clive. "Smith's mum, I mean."

He was yawning again. "Maybe – uh – five minutes ago? Now, about Judith, I was just – "

"Can you get dressed and give us a lift?" I said.

"Why should I? I was planning on going back to bed."

"Do you want Judith to come with you on Saturday?" I said. "Or not? It's all the same to me."

"Where do you want to go?"

It was a reasonable question but I didn't have an answer for it. I hesitated, thinking it would be fairer to level with him. Then I had an idea that gave levelling with him a practical attraction. There was no time to consult the others about it or to consider how best to present it. So I plunged straight in.

"If you want me to help you with Judith, you've got to keep your mouth shut. Okay? Jenny's on the run from the police. She's an illegal immigrant and we're trying to get her out of the country."

"Uh huh," Clive said. "No problem."

I had the feeling that if I'd said that Jenny was a carnivorous pumpkin with a taste for human flesh, he'd have reacted in exactly the same way.

Smith said, "Now, wait a minute, Chris."

I ignored her. "Your lodger – Sue – she's just come back from the Caribbean, right? So she's got a passport. Do you think she might let Jenny borrow it?"

Clive shrugged. "I don't know where Sue is. I think Mike said they'd be back on Sunday."

117

The towel started to slide down his hips. He grabbed it just in time.

"It's not Sue we want, exactly," I said. "It's her passport."

There were two seconds of dead silence. Then Clive produced his miracle.

"No problem. You want it right now?"

"Please. Er – she wouldn't mind?"

"Why should she?"

I could think of several reasons but now was not the moment to mention them. Clive went into the bedroom Sue shared with Mike and heaved the mattress off the bed. The polystyrene head rolled on to the floor.

"This woman," Jenny said with something that might have been hope in her voice, "she looks like me?"

"Well, she's not identical," I said, which was the sort of understatement that isn't very different from a downright lie. "But she's black, about five-six or seven, and she's in her twenties."

Clive appeared in the bedroom doorway with two passports in his hand. "You want Mike's as well?"

I shook my head. No one can say that Clive isn't generous. He threw me Sue's passport. It contained a colour photograph, which showed the orange wig to advantage. Sue wore green earrings that dangled down to her shoulders. Round her neck was a necklace the size of a small breastplate. She was smiling roguishly at the camera.

"But she's nothing like me," Jenny said.

"I know," I said. "That's the beauty of it. She doesn't look like you but there's no reason why you shouldn't look like her. Is there?"

"This evening?" Clive said. "Are you sure?"

It was three hours later and we were having a sandwich in one of the open-air restaurants in Covent Garden. The

118

place was stuffed with tourists in search of the real London.

"Yeah," I said. "She said she wouldn't make any promises about Saturday but she agreed to talk about it. You meet her after work. She said something about going to a cocktail bar in Old Compton Street."

"The Black Dahlia," Clive muttered automatically. "But how did you do it?"

"Well, it wasn't easy, I'll tell you that."

I didn't want to go into the details. It had been an unsavoury business. I'd used a mixture of bribery and blackmail, which is the only tactic that cuts any ice with my sister. Just after Christmas we'd gone halves on a two-inch portable colour TV; one of my mates from school had found it underneath a lorry and was selling it for about a third of the manufacturer's recommended retail price. For Clive's sake, I'd made over my fifty per cent share to Judith. As for the blackmail, I'd threatened to come and see her at her office. The very idea of that made her have hysterics over the phone. Even so, I was surprised she agreed with so little fuss to see Clive. Maybe I'd been stupid to mention the TV. I've a sneaking feeling she was just waiting for an excuse to see him again – anything that would save her losing face.

"I haven't shaved," Clive said. "I've got to change, plan my strategy."

"It's only just after two," I said. "You've got plenty of time. Look, there's Smith and Jenny."

There was a definite cut in the volume of noise around us. Forks stopped moving. Conversations faltered in midsentence. One of the tourists reached for his video camera but his wife wouldn't let him use it.

I've noticed before that the thrill of creation can have an effect like alcohol: it makes you feel a little larger than life, a little more powerful than everyone else. You're deluding yourself, of course, but, as with alcohol, it's fun while it lasts.

For an instant, that was the feeling I had when I saw them, each carrying a new suitcase, zig-zagging among the tables towards us. If I hadn't known about the wig I wouldn't have recognized Jenny.

Clive said: "*Jesus*!"

It wasn't that she looked sexy or beautiful. But she was exotic – like a tropical bird surrounded by drab city pigeons. The orange wig, the yellow top and the short red skirt came from Sue's wardrobe. I heard later that Smith had chosen and paid for everything else. They'd taken most of Oxford Street apart in their quest for the right accessories for Jenny's new personality.

The weirdest thing of all was the fact that Jenny was obviously enjoying it. You could tell by the way she moved: she was strutting, not walking. She didn't just look like someone else, she felt like it, too.

"I still don't look much like Sue," Jenny said as she sat down. Her personality change hadn't made her less grumpy.

Clive put on a pair of dark glasses.

"Maybe not in detail." Smith was trying not to laugh. "But the overall effect is just fine."

"I don't think anyone's going to look too closely at your face," I said.

There were so many cosmetics on it that very little of the face was visible.

"We had the make-up done professionally," Smith said. She looked at Jenny with proprietorial pride. "Not bad, huh? Did you get the ticket?"

I nodded. Clive and I had visited the British Airways office in Regent Street.

"18.45 out of Heathrow, Terminal One," I said, feeling like a travel agent myself. "Arrives Geneva 21.15. It's a Boeing 757. Minimum check-in time from the concourse is half an hour."

We had to shut up because a waiter came up to take their order. Smith smiled at me. I guessed she was feeling as relieved as I was. This business wasn't over yet but at least we were through the worst of it. Jenny had a ticket and a passport, plus a new name and new appearance to go with it. The police were still looking for the Jenny who'd been at Youlgreave Barton. They knew, of course, that we were with her and that we'd been at Clive's in the morning. But we weren't there now. They had four and a half hours to find us in a city of seven million people. For once the odds were in our favour.

Smith nudged my arm. "Jenny would be safer without us."

"I know. Frances must have given our descriptions to the cops."

"Don't leave me," Jenny said unexpectedly. "Please."

What it is to be needed.

Clive was looking vacant again. He'd been frowning at his glass of lager for the last five minutes. He looked up, "Chris, what time does Judith finish work today?"

"How should I know?" I wasn't best pleased at the interruption. "Same time as usual, I guess."

"But it varies. I mean, think how she'd feel if I wasn't waiting. It'd be terrible for her."

He sounded really upset by the pain he might be causing her. Personally I could cope with the idea quite easily. Clive is so stupid. Lately he's allowed Judith to make all the decisions. He should try to be more masterful with her – I've told him that. My sister is bossy enough as it is without him making it worse. Let her wait for him: it would do her a world of good. If he lies down and acts like a doormat she's just going to wipe her feet on him. Right now I had far more important things to worry about.

"Then why don't you phone her?" I snapped. "Ask her yourself."

He gnawed his lips for a bit. Then he lolloped off like an eager rabbit to find a payphone. I hope I never get like that.

While he was gone we tried to sort out what to do with Jenny. She just didn't want to be alone. We were still at it when Clive lolloped back, beaming all over his face. He'd had quite a long chat with Judith and for the first time in two weeks he felt their relationship might actually have a future. He told us all about how sensitive she was until I wanted to scream. Then he said he was going home to get changed. I told him he couldn't do that because the police would probably be waiting for him.

"For me?" he said. "But why?"

Once again I explained – very slowly and very simply – that the cops were looking for Jenny. His face grew more and more gloomy. It wasn't the police that worried him – what upset him was the thought that Judith might have to see him in yesterday's socks and with an unshaven chin. I worked on him for ten minutes, at the end of which he'd agreed to buy a razor and any clothes he needed and go and glamourize himself in a public lavatory. Smith offered to pay for the clothes but Clive waved the offer aside. To give him his due he isn't mean with his money.

But I felt mean as he walked away, because I was so glad to see the back of him. We couldn't have managed without him. He still had to explain to Sue what had happened to her passport, her wig and her clothes. Jenny had promised to post them back; I hoped she would.

We spent another quarter of an hour at the restaurant, trying to work out what to do. The trouble was, we were all so tired – none of us was up to making decisions, even easy ones. Finally we agreed to walk to Leicester Square and put in a few hours in a cinema. Sleeping through a movie had its attractions. Then we'd get a taxi to Heathrow, or go there by tube.

In front of the Covent Garden church a shifting crowd surrounded a clown on stilts who was juggling ninepins. As we pushed our way through towards King Street a tall man suddenly stepped in front of Jenny. He was wearing

122

sunglasses, a loose white jacket and very clean jeans; he looked like a tourist – Dutch, maybe, or American.

"Thank God I've found you," he said to Jenny. He had a gentle voice and a nice smile to go with it. "Come on. We need to talk."

He was the sort of guy who makes my sister drool: dark-haired, with chiselled features – just like the hero of a pre-war film.

"Who are you?" Jenny said, backing away from him.

He bent down and whispered. "Underground Railroad. Controller, south-east region."

"How – how did you find me?"

Jenny sounded slightly breathless. I wondered if my sister wasn't the only one who liked suave, romantic types.

"Our intelligence section is pretty good. We'd better get going." He smiled down at her. "There's a lot we need to sort out."

"But we've already arranged – "

"We'll talk on the way. This is too public."

Not just suave: masterful with it. Clive should take lessons from him. Jenny held out her hand for the second suitcase, which I'd been carrying.

"Here, let me take that." The bloke grabbed the case from me and began to pull Jenny away from the knot of people around the juggler. He glanced back at me and Smith. "Thanks for your help. It'll be safer if we don't involve you any more."

"Yeah, thanks," Jenny said – casually, as though we'd done nothing more important than tell her the way to the nearest tube station.

It was all happening too fast. How had the guy recognized Jenny? How did the Underground Railroad even know we were in London? I had a sour taste in my mind because Jenny was so keen to junk us now we'd outlived our usefulness to her. It made me feel like a disposable Good Samaritan: use once and throw away.

"Wait," Smith said. "Did Frances tell you where to find us?"

He nodded. He was concentrating on edging himself and Jenny through a coachload of Japanese.

"*Listen*, will you?" Smith touched his sleeve. "Frances is working for the police."

That stopped him. His face went sort of rigid, as if he were trying to hide his surprise.

"It's true," Jenny said.

"That means you're at risk," Smith said. "So's your whole organization. Leave Jenny with us. She'll be safer."

"You don't have to worry about Frances," the man said. "I'll take care of her. Now, come on."

Jenny frowned. "But what's she up to?"

"Right now? Nothing. We've neutralized her."

It didn't make sense: Frances must have gone to the police not the Underground Railroad when she'd traced us to Clive's. In any case this guy hadn't known the truth about Frances until we'd told him – so why had the Underground Railroad "neutralized" her?

"How do we know you're from the Underground Railroad?" I blurted out.

"Oh, for God's sake. Just back off, will you?" He bent towards me and suddenly he wasn't nice and gentle any more. "You don't understand what's happening. Leave it to the grown-ups, okay?"

He jerked his head at me to emphasize the last sentence. The sunglasses slipped a little way down his nose. The sunlight slanted across his face. There was a band of bleached hair between the two strongly-marked eyebrows.

I looked at Smith. "That's right," I said in a voice that wobbled like a bowl of jelly. "He's not a cop. But he's not Underground Railroad either. It's our old mate Mr Viljoen."

The suitcase he was carrying hit the ground. The next thing I knew, he had one arm round Jenny; the other hand was in his jacket pocket; and he was poking something in the pocket into Jenny's waist.

None of us moved.

The clown was still juggling away. Two of the Japs were

videoing him. There were hundreds of people – laughing, talking, walking and guzzling – within a few yards of us. Someone was playing "Tipperary" on an accordion. This was Covent Garden on a sunny Wednesday afternoon, at the height of the tourist season. It was all wrong. Viljoen and his gun, Jenny and Smith and me: we were on a different planet from everyone else.

"You two kids," Viljoen said quietly, "will walk in front. Hold hands. Each of you carry a case. We'll be right behind you. And no one does anything stupid. All right. Turn round. Off we go."

He didn't need to spell out what would happen if we disobeyed. The four of us walked slowly past the church and turned into Henrietta Street. Smith's hand felt cold but sweaty. My body was shaking. Okay, I thought, Viljoen's going to kill Jenny. He'd rather do it in private but if necessary he'd do it in public. We knew that he wasn't afraid of taking chances.

But what about us? I remembered the Balaclava he'd worn and realized why we were so important to him: we were the only people who'd seen his face.

He stopped beside a navy-blue Toyota Landcruiser with a parking ticket on the windscreen. Viljoen gave Jenny the keys.

"Get in. You're driving. Kids in the back."

We scrambled in. The car was like an oven. The space between the front and back seats was filled with something that looked like a roll of carpet covered with an old blanket. As I wriggled across the seat I kicked aside the edge of the blanket. There was a flash of red, silky material.

That red dress makes her look like a stuffed tomato.

Smith had seen it too. We both looked at Viljoen, who was sitting in the front passenger seat. He gave us one of his trustworthy smiles. I really think he was enjoying himself.

"Like I told you," he said. "Frances has been neutralized."

I wondered if "neutralized" was just another way of saying "killed". By now I'd stopped shivering. Instead my stomach seemed to have a block of ice inside it. I didn't want to think about dying or people getting killed. I wasn't the only one.

"I get it," Smith said in a strained, bright voice. "You came back to get Frances this morning. You didn't have any choice – you figured she was the only person who would know what had happened to Jenny. And when you caught up with her, she wasn't at the Mill, she was in a phone box."

"How do you now that?" Viljoen said.

"Because we talked to Clive, the person she was calling. Then you persuaded her to cooperate and brought her to London. You needed her so Jenny would think you were Underground Railroad. But we weren't at Clive's. So you tried all the other numbers in Chris's diary."

"Including Judith's work number," I interrupted. "Just after Clive had rung her. And he must have told her we were in Covent Garden."

"And Judith told you. Who did you say you were? My father?"

Viljoen grinned at her. "You got it in one. You're bright kids, I give you that. Let's go. I've already got a parking ticket. I don't want to get clamped."

It was a slow, hot journey. He took us east, keeping north of the river. For a while we drove along the A13. I don't know this end of London well. I think it was in Stepney that Frances began to twitch beneath the blanket. The block of ice was still there but it grew a little smaller.

Jenny drove carefully and well. I wished to God she'd had the sense to drive badly. It would have been so easy for her to ram a bus, or jump a red light in front of a patrol car, or just to switch the hazard-warning lights on. Anything to get the police interested in us. But she was in a trance. Occasionally the orange wig twitched sideways as she glanced down at the gun on Viljoen's lap.

I edged along the seat and got my fingers on the handle. The next time we stopped I tried to open the door. It wouldn't budge.

"Child locks," Viljoen said. He'd angled the mirror in the sun visor so he could see what I was doing. "You can only open the rear doors from the outside. Better safe than sorry, eh?"

We passed signs to the Blackwall Tunnel on our right. Just after that Viljoen ordered Jenny to turn left off the A13. I didn't know exactly where we were – East Ham or West Ham: somewhere like that. Viljoen discouraged conversation. Finally we turned into a long, narrow cul-de-sac.

Rows of grimy little houses faced each other across the street. Their windows and doors were blocked. Even the squatters had moved out. We stopped at the far end in front of a chainmesh fence. It was about 12 feet high and it had a frill of barbed wire along the top. On the other side of the fence was a building site like a long-lost World War I battlefield.

"Open the gates, Chris." Viljoen passed me a key. "Remember that your girlfriend's staying here."

"It's not the sort of thing you forget," I said, "is it?"

I lowered down the window to open the door from the outside. I staggered to the fence. There were several faded notices on it – DE BLOOM PROPERTIES, ALL VISITORS *MUST* REPORT TO THE SITE OFFICE and THIS SITE IS PROTECTED BY GUARD DOGS. I unlocked the gates and pulled them just wide enough apart to let the car in.

The Toyota jolted past me and stopped. Viljoen told me to relock the gates behind them. He leant out of the window to watch. For an instant I was tempted to run down that straight, dusty road. Then I realized that for 200 yards I'd be waiting for a bullet to hit my back. Or

Smith's head. I couldn't do it. I felt so angry and so powerless to do anything about it that I could have sat down and cried. Instead I did as I was told.

"Get back in," Viljoen said.

The Landcruiser bumped slowly along a track that led deeper and deeper into the wasteland. We passed a mobile site office with smashed windows but there was no machinery around – no sign that anyone actually worked here for a very long time.

Only the weeds were alive. Everywhere there were heaps of hard, dry earth, small hills of sand and gravel, and piles of pipes and concrete blocks. Scraps of wood, empty drums and rolls of rusting wire were scattered like forgotten toys in a giant's sandpit.

I remember thinking that someone with a lot of money must want Jenny dead. Viljoen smelled expensive: all that dedication and all those specialized skills wouldn't come cheap. He'd been able to hire Brian and Sammy Jo to help him. He had the Toyota with its CD player and carphone. He had guns and walkie-talkies. He seemed to have exclusive use of this very private wilderness. It made me sick to think that someone was squandering all these resources on killing one defenceless person. There must be better things to do with money.

The track went downhill into a sort of shallow saucer. At the bottom was a great rectangle of cracked concrete. A network of trenches spread out from one end of the rectangle – maybe they were for drainage or more foundations.

"Okay," Viljoen said. "This is where we stop."

Jenny braked and switched off the engine.

"Put your right hand through the steering wheel," he told her. "That's it. Now put your wrists together – no, keep your left arm outside the wheel. Good girl."

He wound parcel tape round her wrists – over and over again. Jenny just sat there, as though this were the sort of thing that happened to her every day. When he'd finished he patted her shoulder. She rested her head against the steering wheel. Her eyes were closed.

It only took a few seconds. Somehow that ridiculous wig and Jenny's borrowed finery made it all the worse. Smith and I sat rigidly in the back. Frances moaned and tried to lift her legs beneath the blanket. Viljoen waved the gun at us.

"I want you two outside."

"Why?" Smith said.

"You'll find out."

We clambered out of the Toyota. Viljoen jumped on to the concrete plinth and beckoned us to follow. He led us along the edge to one of the corners. Below us was the network of trenches.

"I'm going to offer you a deal," he said. "I've got nothing against you two, or even Frances. But Jenny is something different. It's business, you know. Nothing personal."

Neither of us said anything.

"Now. This site's being reactivated next month. First thing they'll do is line these trenches with concrete. I want you to dig me a hole. In return you get to stay alive – you and Frances. If not, I dig the hole myself. But in that case it'll have to be a larger hole. You with me?"

I didn't believe him. Making us accessories to Jenny's murder didn't stop us being witnesses to it as well.

"You mean you'd let us go?" Smith said. "Really?"

Viljoen smiled. "If I can. In a few hours I'll be out of the country. Of course I'd have to make sure you couldn't talk to anyone beforehand."

"Well, that sounds fair enough," Smith said, opening her eyes very wide. "But how will you do it?"

I thought she'd gone too far, especially when she batted her eyelashes at him. Couldn't he tell that she was taking him for a ride? Did he really think we were stupid enough to dig our own graves and let him shoot us when he'd finished?

But Viljoen was still smiling at her. I thought of the bleached hair and suddenly understood: he thought he could walk over any woman and they'd sit up and thank him for it. Smith had been right after all: his vanity was important: it was the only weapon we had left.

"There's a shed at the other end of the site. I'll lock the three of you in there. I'll leave you some water and food, don't worry. You'll get out eventually. But it'll take you a little time."

"Well." Smith turned to me. "I guess we can't say no. Can we, Chris?"

I nodded. If I ran one way and Smith ran the other, he could only shoot one of us. And then he'd have to track down the survivor. But if he hadn't much time to play with, the survivor had a sporting chance of surviving a little longer.

"That's great," Viljoen said. "We'll get the shovels. They're in the back of the car."

We strolled back with him. He kept a few paces away from us and he was still holding the gun; but he was much more relaxed than I'd seen him before.

"It makes things easier when people are sensible," he said to Smith. "A little cost-benefit analysis – that's all it takes."

She was walking alongside him with her hands deep in her pockets, looking up at his face. You'd have thought he was her favourite uncle or something. Left to myself, I wouldn't have waited any longer to make a run for it. But Smith had to have a reason for her groupie act.

I could see a blob of orange behind the windscreen of the Toyota. It reminded me of one of Clive's cuddly toys. If I have to die for someone, I thought, I wish it could be someone I cared for. Then I remembered Gisburn acting like a comic-strip hero: not so much because he liked Jenny but because his God didn't approve of what Caesar was doing to her.

Viljoen swung the tailgate open and stood back. "Get

131

the shovels out," he said to me. "The earth's loose – you shouldn't need a pick."

His attention was mostly on me. He'd backed away from the Landcruiser – just in case I was tempted to try something with a shovel or the pick – but the gun was hanging loosely in his right hand, pointing downwards.

Smith was sidling closer to him.

I got my hands round one of the shovels. "Hey," I said, turning my head. "What's happened to Frances?"

Viljoen took a step towards me. Smith tugged her hand out of her pocket. She was holding something cupped in the palm.

"No, it's okay," I said. "She's still there."

I straightened up, holding the shovel. In a blur of movement Smith's hand swooped up and smacked into Viljoen's face. For an instant I thought she was aiming at the bleached patch between the eyebrows.

Viljoen screamed. He dropped the gun. His fingers dug at his eyes as if he wanted to claw them out. He rocked forwards and backwards.

And all the time he screamed and screamed.

CHAPTER FIFTEEN

There was only one thing to do. I didn't want to do it. But I did it all the same.

I lifted the shovel above my shoulder and swung it like an axe against the side of Viljoen's head. Just the weight was enough – I added hardly any force to the blow. The curved rim of the blade thudded into him. The shovel tried to jump out of my hands. Viljoen keeled over on top of a clump of nettles. Smith crouched down and picked up the gun.

He was still conscious but most of the fight had gone out of him. The screams became moans. His hands pawed at the enflamed eyes.

I sneezed. "Gisburn's pepper?" I said.

"I think it's chilli powder. Get the parcel tape."

I ran round to the passenger side of the Toyota. The roll of tape was lying on the seat. Jenny didn't move as I opened the door. Her eyes were closed.

"Water," Viljoen said when I got back. "For God's sake, get me water. The white container by the shovels."

"Hold out your hands first," I said. "Wrists together."

He was trying to get up. It was almost painful to watch him.

"Stay where you are," Smith said.

He just carried on regardless.

"You heard me."

Smith pulled the trigger. I almost dropped the shovel. The bullet ricocheted off the concrete. It made a whining noise, like a vicious winged insect.

Viljoen held out his hands. I bound his wrists together and then did the same for his ankles.

"Please," he said. "Water."

Smith was already there with the container and a bunch of tissues from her pocket. She swabbed his eyes carefully and even gave him a drink. Then she picked up the gun and we backed away from both Viljoen and the Toyota. Jenny still hadn't moved.

Smith leant against me – so suddenly that at first I thought she'd fainted. I put my arms round her. We stood like that, not talking and barely moving. She was trembling but gradually she grew still.

Everything was very quiet. It was as if we were the last people left on a battlefield. Only one thing mattered. We were alive.

"You do a lot of shooting then?" I said, as casually as I could.

"Only when I have to. My father taught me."

Then she remembered that the gun was digging into the small of my back and that she'd left the safety catch off. That was the end of our magical moment. I looked at my watch. It was only 4.00 p.m. We still had three problems to deal with.

"We take Jenny to Heathrow?" I said.

Smith nodded.

"We'll have to hurry if we want to beat the rush-hour traffic."

"And the other two?"

"Leave them here," I said. "Let the police sort them out."

"I want to talk to Frances first."

"There's nothing to say to her, is there?"

"It's not for our sake," Smith said. "My father's."

"Okay. But keep it short."

We went over to the Toyota. Smith pulled the blanket off Frances and undid the gag that covered her mouth. She stared at us. We stared at her hands – at the tips of her fingers, which were red and swollen. Frances hadn't made it easy for Viljoen, and he hadn't made it easy for her.

"We're going to take Jenny away," Smith said. "But we'll call the police and tell them where to find you. We've tied up Viljoen. Do you want some water?"

Silly question. We pulled Frances on to the seat and fetched the water. Smith held the container to her lips. Some of the water ran down her chin and on to the red dress.

"Why did you do it?" Smith said. "I really want to know. Did you need the money or something?"

Frances ran her tongue across her lips. Then the words tumbled out of her in a rush – jostling together as though they'd been trying to escape for a long time.

"Money's got nothing to do with it," she said. "Can't you understand the Underground Railroad is breaking the law? The law's the only thing between us and chaos. People who live here and in the States – they don't know what chaos is. But I know."

She stopped abruptly, squeezing her lips together as though trying to prevent more words escaping. She was looking at me, not Smith, and something in her face reminded me of Jenny. I think it was despair – the same sour blend of fear and hopeless anger that Viljoen had made me feel today.

"Something happened to you, didn't it?" I said; and for the first time when speaking to her I wasn't nervous in any way. "What was it?"

"All right," Frances said furiously. "You really want to know? I was born in Rhodesia – we had a farm near Bulawayo. One day the guerrillas came. They called themselves freedom fighters and they acted like drunken bandits. I was in England, at school. But my parents were there, and my little sister."

The tears were pouring down her cheeks. How would Gisburn have coped with this, I wondered? Where did God and Caesar fit? Which God? Which Caesar?

"I wanted to do something," Frances went on in the same cracked, angry voice as before. "Something to *help*,

135

to make up for them dying. This isn't revenge. I had a client a year or two back who was obviously an illegal immigrant. So I talked to the police about him. It was my *duty*. They suggested that I infiltrate the Underground Railroad."

"Does my father know?" Smith said.

"He knows what happened on the farm, about me helping with the Underground Railroad. But not – well, not about the rest of it."

Smith sighed – I think with relief. She said: "So you fooled him too? Good for your image, was he?"

"It wasn't like that at all," Frances said wearily. "I promise you that."

Without warning the orange wig moved. Jenny raised her head from the steering wheel and turned round. Her make-up was a mess.

"I'll tell you what it's like," she said. "It's like treachery. And if I had that gun, I'd kill you and I'd kill Viljoen. That would be a kind way for you to die."

"Killing people won't help," Smith said. "You should know that if anyone does."

"We should get going," I said. All this talking was making me uncomfortable. I didn't want to feel sorry for Frances any more than I wanted to dislike Jenny. The next thing I knew I'd be telling myself that Viljoen was just a craftsman trying to earn an honest living. Why do people always have to confuse things? The better you know them, the more complicated they become.

The great thing about activity is that it stops you asking yourself unanswerable questions.

Jenny had quietened down, so we separated her from the steering wheel and gave her the rest of the water. But first Smith locked the gun in the glove box and gave me the keys.

We hauled Viljoen into one patch of shade and Frances into another. That parcel tape is terrific stuff. I finished

136

the roll on Viljoen and by the end of it he looked like an Egyptian mummy. Once he tried to bite me. After that he offered me a bribe. Finally he stared at me with his bloodshot blue eyes.

"So long, mate," I said. "Next time, why don't you pick on someone your own size?"

He spat at me but missed. The spittle dribbled down his chin.

Between them Smith and Jenny repaired Jenny's appearance. Her clothes were a bit rumpled, and her face had lost its high-gloss finish, but by the end of the overhaul she looked more like Sue than herself.

There was a moment's panic when we thought we'd left the key to the gates in Viljoen's pocket. It was Jenny who told us he'd left it in the ashtray.

We drove down the track, through the gates and into the cul-de-sac. I sat in the front, navigating; I'd found an A-Z London Street Atlas in the glove box. Smith was curled up in the back seat. Every now and then I looked at her in the make-up mirror in the middle of the sun visor. We had all the windows open and I couldn't stop smiling because of the fresh, cool air and Smith in the seat behind me.

At the end of the cul-de-sac I checked the name of the road. We pulled over while I found our position on the map. Fremantle Street, E13. It's nice to know where you are.

I knew there was still plenty to worry about: missing the flight, for example, and the police. But there would always be other flights; and now we knew that Frances hadn't had time to talk to Anthorn, the police weren't so much of a danger.

The traffic wasn't a problem until we got to Aldgate. Then it began to clog up. I suggested we let the train take the strain. We crawled along to Holborn Viaduct and left the Toyota on a double-yellow line in Southampton Row.

"What about *that*?" I said, pointing at the glove box.

"I don't want it," Smith said. "It's Viljoen's car so it's Viljoen's gun. Let him explain it."

We locked the car and dropped the keys down the nearest drain.

Holborn's on the Piccadilly Line: we got a tube directly to Heathrow. And I mean directly: the train was waiting on the platform as though providence had put it there solely for our convenience. We were just in front of the main rush hour so we all got seats. When we got on board, Jenny had a dose of paranoia: she insisted we didn't travel side by side; and she was even uneasy about being in the same carriage as us.

"Suppose it all goes to plan," I said to Smith as the train rushed through the darkness towards Leicester Square. "What then?"

"Back to real life, I guess. I don't think we've got anything to worry about from the cops."

"You'll want to let your dad know you're okay. And then we have to do something about Frances and Viljoen. Maybe we should ring Anthorn from the airport. He could deal with it all. And then . . ."

I ran out of words and wriggled my eyebrows at her instead.

"If you got a suggestion," Smith said, "why don't you just go right ahead and say it?"

"Well, I just happen to have these Paul Anders tickets in my pocket."

She started to laugh.

We reached the airport in time. Smith and I followed Jenny up the escalators at a discreet distance. She checked in her cases. No one behind the desk batted an eyelid at her. Maybe orange wigs were always flying in and out of Heathrow.

Passengers for Flight BA732 to Geneva were already going through to the departure lounge. I thought Jenny would go through with them, without a backward glance.

But she turned and came towards us. She held out her hand to Smith.

"I should have thanked you both before," she said gruffly. "It's not easy sometimes."

I didn't understand what she meant.

But Smith said: "Always being on the receiving end?"

Jenny nodded. "You understand? I didn't think you would."

"I hope it works out in Geneva."

"Me, too," I said.

As Jenny shook my hand, I had this bleak feeling that we hadn't changed anything. She was still afraid. She was still on the run. Someone still wanted to kill her. All we'd given her was a little more time and somewhere else to run to.

"Will you let us know what happens?" Smith said. "Send us a postcard or something."

"If I can. And there's a lot of things I'd like to ask you."

"Like what?" Smith opened her shoulder bag and began to write her address on a page torn from Frances's Filofax.

"Like how did you know I existed? How did you know I was at Youlgreave Barton?"

"*Would passengers for Flight BA732 to Geneva please go through to the departure lounge.*"

"Chris took a photo of the house on Monday. You were in it, on the other side of the window. I've got it here somewhere."

She gave Jenny the address and scrabbled around in her bag.

"I was trying a double exposure, you see," I explained. "I didn't realize you were in it until we had it developed. If you want, you can keep the print. A sort of souvenir."

"Here it is." Smith handed Jenny the photo. "Look, you can just see your face in the top window on the left. You see it? Behind the glass in the lower lefthand corner."

"Would passengers for Flight BA732 to Geneva please go through to the departure lounge."

"I got to go." Jenny was staring at the print and frowning. "But that can't be me. I never went in that room. I was on the other side of the house." She stuffed the photo in her bag and gave us both a smile. "I'll keep it anyway. Souvenir of you two. Take care."

We watched her walking across the concourse. Whatever she was feeling, that outfit made her look jaunty. A security man was watching her too, but not in a professional way; he was grinning slyly to himself.

"I hope to God she makes it," I said.

Smith said nothing but she took my hand. We stood there until the orange wig had disappeared. Then she looked up at me.

"You got to admit I was right," she said.

"What about?"

"About the face at the window. Think about it logically. If it wasn't this Jenny, it must have been the other one. Some ghost, huh?"

Run With the Hare

LINDA NEWBERY

A sensitive and authentic novel exploring the workings of an animal rights group, through the eyes of Elaine, a sixth-form pupil. Elaine becomes involved with the group through her more forceful friend Kate, and soon becomes involved with Mark, an Adult Education student and one of the more sophisticated members of the group. Elaine finds herself painting slogans and sabotaging a fox hunt. Then she and her friends uncover a dog fighting ring – and things turn very nasty.

£2.50 □

Hairline Cracks

JOHN ROBERT TAYLOR

A gritty, tense and fast-paced story of kidnapping, fraud and cover ups. Sam Lydney's mother knows too much. She's realized that a public inquiry into the safety of a nuclear power station has been rigged. Now she's disappeared and Sam's sure she has been kidnapped, he can trust no one except his resourceful friend Mo, and together they are determined to uncover the crooks' operation and, more importantly, find Sam's mother.

£2.50 □

ARMADA

The Pit

ANN CHEETHAM

The summer has hardly begun when Oliver Wright is plunged into a terrifying darkness. Gripped by fear when workman Ted Hoskins is reduced to a quivering child at a demolition site, Oliver believes something of immense power has been disturbed. But what?

Caught between two worlds – the confused present and the tragic past – Oliver is forced to let events take over.

£2.50 ☐

Nightmare Park

LINDA HOY

A highly original and atmospheric thriller set around a huge modern theme park, a theme park where teenagers suddenly start to disappear . . .

£2.50 ☐

ARMADA

All these books are available at your local bookshop or newsagent, or can be ordered from the publisher. To order direct from the publishers just tick the title you want and fill in the form below:

Name _____

Address _____

_____

Send to: HarperCollins Children's Cash Sales
            PO Box 11
            Falmouth
            Cornwall
            TR10 9EN

Please enclose a cheque or postal order or debit my Visa/Access –

            Credit card no:
            Expiry date:
            Signature:

– to the value of the cover price plus:
UK: 60p for the first book, 25p for the second book, plus 15p per copy for each additional book ordered to a maximum charge of £1.90.

BFPO: 60p for the first book, 25p for the second book plus 15p per copy for the next 7 books, thereafter 9p per book.

Overseas and Eire: £1.25 for the first book, 75p for the second book. Thereafter 28p per book.